Mutant Superhero Zombie Killing Disco Cheerleaders from Outer Space (with Uzis)

D E McCluskey

D E McCluskey

Mutant Superhero Zombie Killing Disco Cheerleaders from Outer Space
(with Uzis)
Copyright © 2019 by D E McCluskey

ISBN
9781914381010

Dammaged Productions

www.dammaged.com

For John Morgan.
When are we going to fix this world, John?
We need to rise, just like the superheroes you introduced me to!

D E McCluskey

1.

THE EXPLOSION LIT the sky as far as the eye could see. The thick, gloomy clouds, suffocating the ground below, were momentarily transformed from dull, dark grey, into bizarre purple maelstroms. They rolled, clashed, and swirled, sparring like heavyweight boxers weighing each other up in the ring. They resembled a thick Irish stout pouring into a pint glass, mixing and settling, mixing and settling.

Forks of lightning burst within the turbulence, streaking through the melancholy, offering brief glimpses of mauve excitement.

It was only early evening, but the rheumy, sickly light had not changed all day. One in the afternoon had looked exactly the same as it did now, at six.

A moment or two in the aftermath of the lightning came the thunder. A heavy, rumbling threat bringing the promise of rain; lots of it.

A storm was coming!

Oldman Loftus was in his field, looking towards the sky. His head was shaking slowly as he assessed the encroaching squall. There was an odd feeling upon him. It came from somewhere deep inside. He could feel it in his stomach, his legs, and the arthritic knuckles of his hands. He had the urge to herd the cattle and sheep indoors, knowing it would be the best thing for them. However, he also knew it would be a fruitless gesture from him. There were too many of them, spread far too wide in the fields, to be practical. Plus, he didn't have a clue how to herd the animals in the first place; that was his wife's job. He'd never been one for physical exertions, but nevertheless, the feeling, not necessarily the intention, was there.

'Looks like this could be a bad one,' he mumbled without taking his eyes from the revolving celestial ballet.

'Aye,' his wife agreed. 'I'm not liking the look of those clouds one bit.' Shaking her head, she turned back to her job at hand, working the massive heap of manure, that was the centre point of the field, with the long pitchfork she was grasping.

As she spread the muck, her husband continued to watch the entertainment above.

Oldman was his real name. Legend had it that he was so ugly at birth, the nurses nicknamed him *Old Man* as a joke. His parents had hoped he would grow out of the wrinkled, ugly face, but he didn't. As he got older, he grew into the ugliness instead, and the nickname stuck.

He picked up the washing basket from where he'd placed it when the purple explosion caught his attention. He gave a second thought to hanging the clothes that were still languishing in the basket. 'I think I'll take these inside and put some more logs onto the fire. They're not going to dry out here. Not today.'

His wife was known locally as Oldgirl. This was mainly just for fun, but mostly it was because she was just as ugly as her husband. How they had gotten together, no-one really knew, or wanted to know for that matter. Gossip in the local bars would sometimes speculate what could have possibly attracted them to each other, but this folly was usually quelled after somebody inevitably mentioned what it must look like when they made whoopie. At that point, the conversation generally ended, rapidly. 'As God made 'em, he matched 'em,' was normally the closing statement of these conversations, and then maybe a quick 'Thank the

Lord' to the fact that they had never entertained the thought of having children.

She watched as Oldman carried the basket toward the house before turning back to her own job. She chuckled and shrugged; she'd never known any different. *The man is as useless as he is ugly*, she thought, plunging the pitchfork back into the stinking pile of muck.

'Let's hope this weather don't cause any disruption to the party tonight,' he mumbled, walking away. 'Them Lions have worked their butts off this season to bring that cup back. Those young-uns deserve to kick their heels and have a bit of fun.'

'And make us a little money too, eh?' Oldgirl chuckled again as she spread another pitchfork of dung over the ground.

The old man nodded. 'Oh aye. It never hurts to make a little bit of the green stuff every now and then.'

As he disappeared into the house chuckling too, Oldgirl stopped what she was doing and looked up into the brooding sky. *He's right about that storm,* she thought. *I don't think I've ever seen clouds like that before.* Once again, she shrugged and returned to her work.

A noise distracted her. She'd expected it to be her husband coming back out of the house, moaning about not being able to get the whites perfectly white in the wash. But it wasn't him. It was an approaching vehicle. It was loud, and it sounded fast. She stopped raking the manure and looked towards the service road that led to their fields. A cloud of dust was rising, it was heading towards them. She smiled a toothless grin and nodded. 'No storm that I remember ever stopped the young-uns from having fun,' she mumbled. She was whistling *'We're in the money'* as she returned to the muck, and the field.

2.

'I DON'T LIKE the look of that sky, man,' the long-haired boy in the passenger seat of the speeding van shouted as he looked out through the dirty, bug strewn windshield.

'What?' the boy in the driver's seat replied, taking his eyes off the road, and looking upward. As he did, the van swerved, causing everyone, and everything, inside to roll with it. A crescendo of crashes exploded from the back as the cymbals and drums, that had been crammed in, banged off the other two band member's heads and bodies.

'Fucking Hell, Keith. Keep your eyes on the road, man. I want to live to see my twenties, you know,' one of the long-haired youths in the back shouted.

'What?' Keith replied again, this time turning towards the back seat, causing the van to swerve even more.

More crashing and yelling ensued.

With wide eyes, Geoff, leaned over from the passenger seat, grabbed the steering wheel, and straightened the direction they were travelling in. 'Let's turn this music down a little, shall we?' he shouted once the vehicle was back, safely, on its original course. He leaned in and twiddled with the knob of the radio that was built into the dashboard.

The music blared almost twice as loud. Quickly realising that the knob had been put on the wrong way, he compensated by turning it in the opposite direction.

'Jesus, man,' Bruce, shouted from the back, holding his hands over his ears. 'I think you just popped a drum.'

'Shut it, dickwad. It can't be any worse than your never-ending tuning,' Chris laughed, removing a cymbal that had almost decapitated his face. 'What were you saying, Geoff? Before Keith almost killed us?'

'I said, I don't like the look of that sky. It looks like there's a storm coming.'

Keith leaned over the dashboard to take another look, and the van swerved again.

Grabbing a handful of his t-shirt, Geoff pulled him back. 'Jesus Christ, where did you learn to drive? The blind school?'

The two band members in the back were swaying with every lurch and bump as the van sped along the dusty road. The numerous instruments stuffed in with them were bouncing off their bodies at every given opportunity. 'Keith, my mom told us to break a leg, not our necks.'

'Are those clouds purple, or have I taken too many ludes?' Keith asked, ignoring the scathing criticisms from his bandmates.

Bruce, who's head was already pushed up against the window, lifted his eyes to look. 'Whoa, they are. They're like, so purple. Oh, man! Just imagine if it rained right now, I could totally write a song about it.'

'What? A song about purple rain?' Geoff scoffed from the front seat. 'Are you on drugs? No-one's going to listen to a song about that shit. Nope, we need to keep our songs about real issues, like getting laid and being loaded all the time.' He turned back to face the road, shaking his head. 'Purple rain? Man, you've got one fucked-up imagination,' he laughed, sparing a glance upwards, towards the clouds, himself.

'Are we nearly there? I think I've got a bass guitar string stuck in my ass,' Chris moaned as he moved the guitar bag away from his face.

'Would that be your *G* string?' Keith asked, laughing.

'It might be your mother's G-string,' Chris retorted, getting laughs from the other band members. Keith shut up then. He didn't have a comeback ready for that one. Silently he fumed as he continued driving at breakneck speed down the dusty road towards the night's gig.

3.

THE CLOUDS ABOVE the small town of Kearney, Arkansas, collided and morphed into nightmarish landscapes of mystery and foreboding. The sun, which had been pushed back, bullied, and beaten, had given up the fight and retreated into hiding around the other side of the Earth's curvature, leaving behind thick, gaseous manifestations as far as the eye could see. The pathetic attempt at day had at last become night, almost within the blink of an eye.

At the exact moment Keith turned on the headlights of the van heading down the dusty old road; and as Oldgirl gave up spreading the piled muck over their fields, tossing her rake into what was left of the heap and walking off with her hands rubbing at the small of her back; and as her husband, Oldman, finished pegging up the last of her delicates on the rack inside the house to dry, before turning his hand to the southern soufflé he was planning for tonight's meal; a single fork of bright purple lightning streaked down from the Heavens.

It's destination, the small town below.

No ripple of thunder accompanied this phenomenon. The only sounds associated with it were a faint sizzle, a cackle, and a small bang as it struck the dusty ground, dissipating through the dry earth.

As if someone had flicked on a switch, the graveyard on Cemetery Road, lit up like a Christmas tree. The illumination occurred only for the merest of seconds, but every tombstone in the gathering shone a bright, almost blinding phosphorescent purple. The stones pulsed brilliantly for a second before the tendrils of light began to retreat inwards, and downwards, towards the soil surrounding them.

This dirt began to vibrate.

A deep purple glow radiated from the minute spaces between the molecules of earth. Then, as quickly as it appeared, it disappeared. The cemetery returned to its usual, peaceful self as if nothing untoward had ever happened.

A single drop of rain dripped from a pregnant cloud above. As it fell, the purple essence within it swirled as if it were oil that refused to mix with the water. When it hit the ground, it seeped into the dusty, dry soil.

It was the first of millions, if not billions, of similar drops to fall that night.

4.

'SUZI'S GOING TO be there, right?' Jason asked as he pulled his Kearney Lions football jersey over his head. 'You told me she's going to be there. *Allegedly*, she's got the hots for me.'

'Don't worry about it. It's all set up, bro,' Brad laughed as he rooted in his sports bag. 'She's head cheerleader, of course she'll be there.'

'Yeah,' a voice shouted from somewhere inside the showers. 'With an emphasis on the *head*!'

There was laughing followed by the slap of palms as whoever was in the shower cheered the joke. He shook his head and chuffed, even though, deep down, his stomach was tying itself up in knots. Lead Quarterback for the Lions, or not, he still got butterflies every time he thought of Suzi. He loved the dazzling smile she offered every time he ran past her with the ball. Her teeth were so white, contrasting perfectly with the beautiful, smooth mocha of her skin. He sighed, lost in the daydream of her tight cheerleader outfit. Marvelling at the way the curves of her breasts made the large white L bend as she jumped. Her smooth, toned legs flexing as she did the splits! The way she sucked on the lollipop she seemed to have almost unlimited supply of. Suzi was, to Jason, hands down the finest sucker of lollipops he had ever seen in his entire life, and he had seen every episode of Kojak. There was just something about the way she rolled the boiled sweet on a stick around her mouth, caressing the ball of candy with her tongue, that gave him chills even thinking about it. However, the finest part about her, the bit that gave him feelings like he needed the toilet every time he saw her, was her large afro haircut.

'Shit, Jason, are you not putting your pants on?' Brad laughed as he snapped Jason's bare behind with his damp towel.

'What?' He looked around, grabbing his stinging butt cheek, with a vacant look on his face, almost as if he had just woken up from a fantastic dream.

'I said, lover boy, you're standing there looking at your pants as if they've just pulled a knife on you, demanding money. Come on, man, snap out of it. Suzi's just a girl.'

Jason laughed. 'Just a girl? Yeah? Like Birdie's just a girl too, eh?'

Brad's face fell. He took in a deep breath through his nostrils and raised his head. 'No, man. Birdie is a true force of nature, baby. The things that girl can do. She makes me feel like I can fly.'

Jason continued to laugh. 'Listen to you. You're there, trying to tell me that Suzi's just a girl, all the while harping on about flying with Birdie. You're a big old fake.'

Brad's eyes snaked around the room as he leaned into his friend. 'Tonight,' he whispered.

'Yeah?' Jason moved in closer.

'Tonight, after the dance, she wants to go *parking!*'

'Parking?' Jason repeated, his eyes wide as the information he had just received filtered through. 'Really?'

'Oh yeah. Her mom and dad are out of town this weekend, and no-one's expecting her home right away.'

Jason held up his hand, and Brad slapped it. 'All right,' he shouted. 'Brad, you're one lucky son-of-a-bitch.'

'I know. I've gone from looking up her skirt at the top of the cheerleader pyramid, to getting myself in there, in no time.'

I wonder how long it'll take me to get that far with Suzi? Jason thought, keeping it to himself.

A series of whoops and shouts came from the showers as four young men, dressed only in towels, exited, shoving each other.

Brad turned back towards Jason. His smile dropped as he leaned in close, acting like he was about to drop a national security secret. 'Do me a solid, would you, man? Don't say anything to the boys. You know what they're like. They'll follow us to the make-out point and ruin everything.'

Jason tipped him a wink. 'Your secret's safe with me,' he lied, knowing that he *was* going to tell the others, and maybe even lead the charge on the car himself.

'What are you fags whispering about in the locker room?' Rob asked. Rob was big and muscular. He looked twenty-five on a good day and at least thirty on a bad one. He was the Lions' muscle. He was one half of the team's defensive tackle, and it was obvious why. Very few runs got past him. He was huge and a lot faster than he looked.

'Just talking about your mom, Rob,' Jason teased to a chorus of jeers from the rest of the room. 'And about how much she likes the defensive tackle, especially on a Saturday night.'

The last part of the comment caused the others to quieten, jockeying for the best positions to watch as this went down.

'Oh, is that right?' Rob asked, his eyebrows raised as he looked at Jason. Jason was almost six feet tall, his smooth, dark skin wrapped around his athletic frame, fitting tightly where it touched. But despite his size, Rob dwarfed him.

'Yeah, that's right,' Jason replied, squaring up, looking his adversary in the eyes.

'Well, your mom lets truckers slip it to her, just to pay for her groceries,' Rob replied to a chorus of cheers and high fives from the guys around him.

'Well, that's probably why you're so fat then. Your mom must get a ton of groceries each weekend,' Jason replied to another swoop of cheers. He could see Rob's face turning red. He could also see his eyes moving rapidly as the big boy's slow brain attempted to conjure another smart reply.

He'd already won.

'Your mom is banged so much in a weekend; she's fitted a lock on her ass to stop it blowing in the wind. She's been in more cockpits than a World War Two pilot. She's so fucking loose...'

'All right, all right... you win, you bastard,' Rob shouted, creasing into laughter.

'Too fucking right, I did,' he shouted responding to all the high fives coming his way. 'Now come on, guys, we've got a dance to get to. Some of those cheerleaders out there want to get past first base, and we're not about to let them down. Not on my watch anyway.' He shot a wink towards Brad, who replied with a stern look before shaking his head.

The others were hollering and shouting again.

Tonight, it was the District Championship Party.

Tonight, they were gods among men. They had won district by a large margin, and they were going to party.

'Hey, guys.' The shouting was interrupted by a late comer to the party. He'd been on the field putting the training materials away.

Jason removed his arm from around Rob's head, stopping giving him a 'nuggie'—rubbing his knuckles through his hair—long enough to see the look on the newcomer's face. 'What's going on, Razor?' he asked, his face now holding only a remnant of its original grin.

'You all need to come and see this. Strangest fucking thing I ever saw,' Razor shouted over the hubbub in the locker room.

'What? Stranger than Rob's mom in the salad isle?' Brad shouted. Everyone stopped what they were doing and turned to look at him. All joviality exited the locker room in an instant. 'What?' he asked, looking around at the rest of the team, who were staring at him with wide, petrified eyes. 'I can't joke about someone's mom like everyone else?'

'What did you say about my mom?' Rob asked. His face was pink, and his hands were clenching, morphing into huge, dangerous, fists.

'I… erm, I was…' Brad stuttered, looking around the room at the faces of his friends, looking for assistance in his tight spot.

None was forthcoming.

'Holy fuck-balls,' Jason shouted as he looked out of the window. 'You guys have got to see this.'

Everyone turned away from the drama that was unfolding, towards where Jason and Razor were stood, their backs to the action. Brad took this moment to duck out, grateful to be away from the bigger boy's wrath, to hide in the shadows of the other lockers.

'What *is* that?' Razor asked. A purple hue had spread across his face, reflecting what he was staring at.

'I've never seen anything like it before, have you?' Jason asked, although the question wasn't directed to anyone in particular. The stunned silence he received, as a reply, told him everything he needed to know. The six boys, all of them champions of the football field, heroes of the Kearney Lions, watched as the sky rolled and pitched with the dirtiest clouds any of them had ever seen.

Jason considered telling Rob that he thought the clouds looked almost as dirty as his mom, but for some reason, the moment didn't seem quite right for a joke.

5.

THERE WERE SIX of them. They were in the main gym, practicing the routine they were scheduled to perform tonight, at the party. They'd been given special permission from the principal to stay in there all day; as she had put it, *it's not every day the home team wins district!*

They'd been there for almost five straight hours, but the perfect performance had continued to elude them all day. 'There's just something missing, ladies,' Suzi shouted as two girls lay on their back before her, exhausted. 'And that something is commitment!' she clapped her hands, encouraging them to dust themselves off, get up, and do better. 'Come on, we need to get this right. We can't have people thinking we're amateurs, with no commitment, right?'

One of the girls was rubbing her rump through the shorts she was wearing underneath her cheerleader skirt. 'Nice! I bet I'm going to have a dirty big bruise on my ass for Brad to kiss better later,' she laughed, blowing hair away from her eyes.

'Birdie, you're a wild one, girl,' Suzi laughed offering her hand to help her up from the floor.

Birdie laughed and accepted the offer. 'So wrong I'm right, baby,' she quipped. 'That pyramid just isn't working, Suzi. Me and Nicky, we just don't feel safe up there.'

Suzi sucked in a breath and looked around at the others. They were all looking back at her, awaiting instruction. The pressure was on to get this right, she was the leader of this squad, she wasn't going to let them down. It was a pressure, and an honour she relished. She thrived on the responsibility, and she would always be there for her girls.

'OK, well, we're going to have to work on this until we *get* it right. There's no way we're going to let our boys down. Pamela, you need to give more support. You're the strongest, so I need you to be solid. Can you give me solid?'

'You know I like it solid, Suzi,' she replied. The rest of the girls began to squeal and laugh.

'Am I surrounded by hoes?' Suzi asked with a theatrical shrug. There were five all of them, all wearing the uniform of the high school cheerleaders, and all of them laughing and nodding. 'On second thoughts, don't answer that. You're all sex crazy,' she concluded, rolling her eyes.

'Oh, right. And you're not, I suppose?' Birdie asked as she wrapped her arm around another girl's shoulders, leaning on her for support. 'And maybe you didn't tell us last night, in The Malt Shop, that you were thinking of going all the way with Jason?'

Suzi felt her dark skin darken a little more as heat flushed through her. 'Well... I, erm...' she stuttered.

'Ah, I thought so,' one of the others answered, jumping up and down in excitement. She surprised everyone by doing several back flips, traversing almost the whole length of the gym in a matter of seconds. 'One of us... One of us... One of us,' she began to chant as she straightened, her arms raised in the air.

'One of us... One of us... One of us...' the others followed suit.

Suzi hung her head low; it wobbled a little as she laughed. 'Betty, is nothing sacred? I told you that in confidence,' she scolded her friend, although her face was filled with humour.

'You should know that by now, girlfriend. *Nothing* is sacred, between friends,' Betty replied, re-joining the group.

'OK, enough joking around. We need to get this shit right, otherwise, we'll be the laughingstock of the school.'

'You do know that it's past six o'clock, don't you?' Nicky, one of the other girls in the squad, asked as she looked at her watch. 'The party starts at eight. We need to be there to get our groove on, sister.'

'Oh, we'll be there,' Suzi nodded. 'And when we are, everyone will *know* we're there.'

Laughing, the girls got themselves into the first positions to run through the routine again.

6.

THE RAIN STARTED to fall.

However, there was nothing normal about it tonight. The drops were larger, and more purple than could be considered *normal*.

They were also glowing.

They didn't seem to be falling as randomly as normal rain did either. In fact, the storm seemed almost localised, following the same path as the freak stripe of lightning that had grounded earlier. The odd water plummeted directly onto the old cemetery at the edge of town. Each droplet landed within the dry, but fertile, soil around the graves. Once it landed, it sunk into the thirsty earth. The odd luminescence of each droplet merged the purple glow inside with the molecules of dirt, transforming it from normal Arkansas soil into something completely different, mud.

This mud sank into the ground, spreading its strangeness towards the things that were buried deep within it.

The slime attached itself to the coffins underground. The purple ooze exuded, effortlessly, through the caskets, searching for gaps, holes, cracks within the wood of the older caskets, or seams between the aluminium of the newer ones. It craved the organic goodness it could sense within the sealed treasure chests.

The cemetery was the final resting place for most of the former residents of the town. Some of them had been interred into these hallowed grounds as long ago as two hundred years, others as recent as a couple of weeks. None of this meant anything to the purple ooze. All that interested it was the organic mass it could sense.

Once inside, the purple secretions slithered towards the heads of the cadavers languishing inside. Tentacles morphed, and extended from the liquid, reaching from the slime, tasting, searching for what it needed.

Brains!

Even residue of brain matter was enough for the glowing globule crawling inside the first coffin. When the scent of brain mass was discovered, the tentacles rose, as if tasting the very air surrounding it. Something caught its attention, and the probe stretched again, hunting for the source of whatever it was it could taste. It lengthened until it came to rest on the cranium of the corpse, lying in state, within the confines.

Something about this discovery excited it, and more probes sprouted, hunting for the source the first had found. Before long, the single blob was joined by others, hundreds, maybe thousands. The illuminated slime was slithering over the body, spreading itself. When the head—or in some of the older coffins, the skull—was completely covered, the invading gunk began to sink until it disappeared.

Nothing else happened then. The ooze was gone, absorbed into the bones, or the rotting flesh, of the corpse within the box.

Peace was once again restored.

Until the cadaver opened its eyes.

7.

AS THEY ARRIVED at the venue, the band were surprised no-one was there to meet them. They pulled the van into the gravelled parking lot of the huge barn that was the location for the gig tonight, the local high school football team's District Championship party.

'Wasn't the promoter guy supposed to meet us here?' Keith asked as he shifted the van into park. He looked out of the window and up into the dark, murky sky. 'Or that Oldman guy? I don't like this.'

'What's the problem?' Geoff asked. 'We don't need that creepy old fella to show us where to set up.'

'I suppose not,' Keith replied, stepping out of the van and stretching. 'Shit,' he spat, looking up at the sky. 'Bruce, I'm thinking you might get what you asked for, man.'

'What?' Bruce asked as he slid the back door open.

'It's starting to rain. Maybe we'll get your purple rain after all,' he laughed. 'We'd better get this shit inside as quick as possible.'

'What's that on the door?' Chris asked as he too stretched his legs. 'It looks like a note.'

'Are you sure the gig's tonight?' Keith asked, looking around the deserted barn and accompanying field. He pulled the collar of his coat up around his neck to keep the drizzling rain from soaking him. 'I'd thought there'd be a welcome committee, or at least someone around, putting decorations up and shit.'

'It's a note from Oldman. It says the keys are underneath a red barrel around the back and that we're to let ourselves in and set up on the stage,' Chris read from the scrap of paper nailed to the door.

'I hope they don't want us to decorate. All I've got in my pocket are a few guitar picks and a pack of condoms,' Bruce shouted from inside the van.

'Well, at least you know one of those items will be used tonight,' Geoff replied, making his way around the large structure to locate the keys.

'Surely, someone's been here and done the hall up. I can't see the District Championship party happening in a dump, can you?' Keith asked as he attempted to peer into one of the dirty windows by the barn's huge double doors.'

'We really are out in the middle of nowhere,' Bruce said regarding his view from the back of the van. He picked up an old newspaper he found on the floor and put it over his head to protect his hair from the rain that was blowing in. The others followed his gaze. In the gloom of the evening, the parking lot was shadowy and miserable, surrounded by fields and trees. The only light breaking the gloom was a faint glow from over a mile away. There was the dark, unlit road they had just driven down, which was the only way in or out, and absolutely nothing else.

'Well, I seriously hope there'll be more people later,' Bruce continued. 'I hate playing to empty rooms.'

'You'd think you'd be used to it,' Keith replied with a smirk. 'What with all that whacking off you do in your bedroom.'

'Yeah, man, hilarious,' Bruce smiled, stepping out of the van. He removed the newspaper from his head and checked the status of the rain.

'What the fuck have you got on?' Chris shouted as the guitarist emerged from the sliding door. 'Jesus! Have you seen this joker?' he asked the rest of the band. 'How did I not see you wearing that when you got in?'

'Because you were too busy looking at yourself in the mirror, trying to fix your receding hair line,' Bruce retorted, lifting his long, sequinned cloak, making sure it didn't get spoilt in the muddy puddles forming on the parking lot ground. As he lifted the garment, he revealed a sparkling pair of glittered platform boots.

'What the fuck are they?' Chris asked again, this time pointing at the ridiculous shoes.

'These, my friend, are all the rage in London. All the bands over there are wearing them. They're called platform boots,' Bruce replied, dancing around the puddles, careful not to get his glittering footwear dirty.

'Bruce, we're not in London, man, we're fucking... here,' Chris replied, gesturing to the whole lot of nothing around them. 'We're about as far away from London as you can get.'

'Well, when you guys go out there tonight in your jeans, engineer boots, and t-shirts, I'll be standing out like the beacon of talent I am.'

'You'll stand out all right, like the first one to get hit in the inevitable punch-up that'll happen later,' Chris finished. 'You look like a reject from Kiss!'

Bruce swooped his cape theatrically and walked off, wobbling slightly on the high platforms, towards the doors. Keith and Chris watched him go.

'I've got the keys,' Geoff shouted, making his way back from around the barn. 'They were under a red barrel like the note said. So, let's start getting the gear in.'

'Can someone bring my stuff in for me please? I don't think I'll be able to carry them in this outfit,' Bruce shouted, opening his cape, revealing the all-in-one, glittering, jumpsuit that matched his boots.

Geoff put his head in his hands. 'What... the fuck... is that?' he asked, gawping at the ridiculousness before him, almost dropping the keys. He was still laughing as he fitted them into the locks and opened the doors.

The wooden entrance creaked open, revealing a small anti-room, nothing more than an unimpressive cloakroom. But there were large double doors opposite him. He made his way through and pushed them open. As they swung, a rush of air hit him. From that rush, Geoff could tell that the room was vast, even though it was dark. He felt around the wall behind the door, his fingers eventually finding the plastic plate on the wall. He flicked the switches, and an electrical hum filled the air. This was followed by an odd strobing effect as the strip lights, high up in the rafters of the room, flickered into life.

'Whoa!' Geoff exclaimed, with his eyes widening.

The rest of the band followed suit.

The walls were white, with a liberal splashing of purple and gold here and there, a tribute to the colours of the Kearney Lions. Decorative bunting adorned the walls, and a huge chandelier had been mounted in the centre of the ceiling. Inside, the hanging lights had been disguised as disco glitter balls. The stage at the far end had been set up with a wall of amplifiers, mic-stands, and a drum kit. The tables between them and the stage were all sporting white tablecloths with purple and gold runners. Along the side of the room, a bar had been set up. Although they knew there would only be soft drinks and punch served, it was still an impressive sight to see.

'Fuck me!' Bruce muttered as he wobbled into the hall. 'I'm going to look glorious up there.'

The rest of the band knew he'd meant to say this to himself, and uttering it aloud had been a mistake, but deep down, they all knew it was true; he *was* going to look glorious up there.

Keith was fuming with himself that he hadn't dressed up too. He had always wanted to shine as much as Bruce. *Drummers just don't get to sparkle as much as guitarists,* he thought with a small pout. For the first time ever, in his musical career, he cursed the day he'd picked the sticks instead of the strings. He made a mental note that tomorrow, with the money he made from this gig, he was going to get himself a show suit. *I'll give that cat out of Kiss a run for his money,* he thought.

'This is awesome,' Geoff muttered, looking around. 'Let's get the gear in and sound-check this mother.'

'Fucking-A,' Chris replied and ran back out to the van.

All the others followed, except Bruce, who was too busy making his way, unsteadily, towards the stage at the end of the room.

'Hey, princess,' Chris shouted as he struggled to bring in bags filled with musical equipment, while flicking wet hair from his face. 'It's pouring down out there, how about helping to get the stuff together?'

Bruce turned and looked at the bass guitarist. He spread his arms wide, making the cloak he was wearing appear like wings. 'Isn't this the business? Tonight, I'll shine. I'll become the legend,' he shouted. 'People will watch me transform. I can feel it!'

'Whatever, dickhead. Go and get your fucking guitars.'

Bruce dropped his arms and looked around the hall. 'OK,' he said, nodding as he hobbled out into the rain, towards the van.

8.

THE RAIN CONTINUED to fall.

For everywhere else in the town, it had only started as a light rain, but in the cemetery, it fell heavy. Big, dark, oily blobs drenched the ground, soaking every inch of the ancient graveyard.

The dry dirt was now a swamp of dark purple mud, seeping and slinking into every grave, every mausoleum, every location where bodies were buried. With purpose, it skulked, seeking the one thing it desired.

Brains!

In the dimness of the pseudo-night, something was happening, something odd and horrifying; shocking even. It was a phenomenon that went against every belief humanity was programmed to believe, either religiously or scientifically.

A constant of life is that the dead stay dead. They are gone, used up, finished. In a few years' time, there would be a saying that something is 'as dead as disco' (although, no-one was saying that right now, as disco was currently *the* in-thing). But once something passed, it never came back.

The phenomenon began with the ground bubbling and gurgling, as if there was a disturbance happening beneath. Like something trying to get *out*.

Not trying exactly, but succeeding.

Heaps of wet earth were being pushed upwards instead of sinking inwards. The purple hue that the rain had caused was casting deep shadows around the graves, silhouettes that looked like they wanted nothing to do with whatever unholy abomination was spewing forth from the disturbances. The faint glow, radiating from the slime, illuminated the eruptions as whatever was escaping was getting closer to the surface.

Not a bird could be heard in the trees, not a fox or rabbit scurried in the undergrowth. The only sound permeating the unnaturally dark graveyard was a subterranean scratching.

Eventually, even that stopped.

Whatever had been coming, was here.

The ground parted and something terrible, and scientifically impossible, escaped the confines of the earth. Something that should never have seen the light of day, or night. Something that, by everything that was holy, and natural, should not even be animated.

Two long decayed fingers emerged from the purple mire.

The fingers looked like they had once been human. They might have once been the dexterous digits of a musician, an engineer, a surgeon. They might have been the same fingers that had once hammered the nails into the very first houses of the settlers who had founded the town. However, these fingers were no longer interested in working with woods, metals, or even plastics. They only had one job to fulfil. As they flexed, flakes of rotted flesh mixed with dirt, fell away, leaving thin, gossamer bridges of purple fluid spanning the gulfs between the decay and the bone.

They found purchase on the slippery dirt just as another set broke the ground next to them. These fingers also found purchase and were soon joined by the rest of the hand. The wet soil gave way, allowing the ground to give birth to its hideous child.

Covered in the filth of ages from its ancient prison and the putrid decay of its own dead flesh, an unholy head surfaced from the maw. What little hair it had was plastered to its scalp, barely covering the patches of exposed cranium where what was left of the flesh had either been eaten, or rotted, away.

There was no nose to speak of, and the mouth was a rictus of age and deterioration. The paper-thin lips were stretched so far across its face that they had ripped in the centre. Grey, but strong, teeth grinned from the ugly, torn orifice, grinding together hungrily. Whatever this abomination was, it was sentient; there looked to be a dastardly malevolent intelligence in its face.

The most unsettling part of this abomination were its eyes, or what passed for eyes. In the deep black recesses where eyeballs would normally reside, there were two glowing, purple lights.

The unhallowed thing turned its head, scanning its surroundings. Using what remained of its skeletal arms, it heaved the rest of its ramshackle body from the earthy prison. Once free, it rolled in the mud before finding a way to sit up. Then, using its arms once again as leverage, the thing began to stand.

The shabby, dirty clothes it wore identified it as male, but this thing would never again be recognised as a man. Apart from its shape, there was very little humanity about it.

It stood shakily on its spindly legs; its movements akin to a ghastly new-born giraffe finding its way in the new and strange world it had been thrust into. Gingerly, it stepped away from the hole it had climbed from and set out on the mission it was here to do.

All around the graveyard, more disturbances were occurring from other graves. Fingers, some as rotten as the first ones, some worse, some no-where near as old, emerged from the increasing number of unholy molehills. Ghoulish faces emerged from the grime. Some were men, some were women, some were children, many of them indeterminate of gender.

They shared a few common characteristics, however. Each of them sported strong, dangerous teeth; and each had glowing purple lights where their eyes should have been. Another characteristic they shared was the single determination in their rotting, flaking faces to carry out the agenda that had caused them to rise from their supposedly eternal slumber.

This agenda was to feed.

9.

AFTER ANOTHER HOUR of practice, a tired Suzi felt they had finally gotten the routine tight. 'So, after the pyramid's done, Birdie, are you sure you're going to be OK doing the back flip from the top?'

Birdie was sat in the corner of the gym stretching her legs, doing her warm-down routine. 'Oh yeah, don't worry about me. I'll have it down tonight. There's no way I'm going to mess this one up.'

'OK then, ladies, I think it's time we got our game faces on and get ourselves in the mood for disco. The boys are going to miss us if we don't.'

'Right on, sister,' Betty whooped as she, too, warmed down next to Birdie.

'We need to get a wriggle on if we're going to get there for the start,' Nicky said, looking at her watch. 'I don't want to keep Kevin waiting any more than he already has been… if you know what I mean!'

Suzi walked past and hip bumped her. 'Let's go and shower, get our war paint on, and get this groove kicking, baby. We're going to need to be at our most dazzling tonight girls. This night might be all about the boys' win, but when we get our scene going, ain't no-one going to be taking their eyes off us!'

There was much screaming and hand slapping as the six girls of the Kearney High School cheerleading squad made their way into the showers.

Forty-five minutes later, they were showered, made-up, and ready to shine. Suzi's hair was big, and as she fluffed it out with her hair pick, it was getting bigger. Wendy was spraying it with an aerosol hair spray.

'Hey, sister, not too much of that now. If Jason's as hot tonight as I think he's going to be, I don't want to be starting any fires I can't put out. You know what I'm saying?'

'Oh, I don't think there is anything to worry about on that score,' Wendy replied. 'One look at you, and he'll be putty in your hands.'

'Let's hope he's not too much putty,' Suzi laughed.

Wendy squealed in delight. 'Oh, you dirty ho,' she teased as she leaned into the mirror that Suzi was looking in, starting to fix her own hair. 'Do you think Razor will even notice my new do?'

'If he doesn't, then that boy is blind,' Pamela snapped as she rubbed lotion into her muscular legs. 'I know my Rob is just going to drop dead when he sees me tonight.'

'If only Hank was as attentive as your Rob,' Betty said, pulling on her sweater.

'Are you joking, girl? That boy has eyes for one thing, and for one thing only,' Suzi said, turning to watch her friend apply lipstick.

'Yeah, football...' Betty quipped, and the girls began to laugh. 'So, Suzi, tonight's the night, yeah? You finally going to let Jason into Suzi Afro's dark delights?'

Suzi grinned; her mocha skin flushed a little darker as she stared into the mirror. 'Does *everyone* know about me and Jason tonight?'

'Erm, yeah,' Pamela replied, cocking her head. 'You've been going on about it non-stop for the last week. It's been why practice was so bad today. Your mind has been on other things, girlfriend.' She leaned in and gave her friend's ribs a tickle.

'Watch my hair…' Suzi shrieked, squirming out of the way of Pamela's attack.

'Oh my God!' Birdie shouted as she walked back into the changing room. 'Have you guys seen the weather out there? It's a frigging tornado, I'm sure of it.'

'It's not a tornado,' Suzi said, getting up out of her seat, fixing the cheerleader outfit she was wearing, straightening it over her curves. *Please, don't let it be a tornado,* she thought.

'Well, it sure does look like one,' Birdie continued. 'See for yourself.' She opened the frosted window so everyone could see the torrents of rain pouring down.

'Aw shit. That's going to ruin my 'do for sure,' Wendy said, fixing her long black hair in the mirror.

'What, and Razor isn't?' Nicky laughed. 'Girl, a bit of water will be *nothing* compared to what he's going to be putting in it later.'

'Nicky!' Wendy said, feigning shock. 'Why do you have to bring everything down to your level?' she asked, turning away from the window.

Nicky pulled a face and grinned. 'Because, sweetheart, when you're sixteen and living in a shithole backwater like Kearney, there isn't anything else to think about.'

'Come on, you two. We need to think about getting to the barn. The party will be over before we even get there,' Pamela said, lifting her coat off the hook. 'We can go in my car. It can fit all six of us. That'll save us time going individually.'

'Great idea. Come on, ladies, let's go and sizzle,' Suzi shrieked grabbing her own coat from the peg and swaggering out of the locker room.

10.

The sound check had been great, and the band were now in the mood for the coming festivities. They knew their audience and knew that disco was going to be the main theme. It was the latest thing, and the kids loved it.

'I hate disco,' Keith moaned as he stood up from behind the kit. 'It's such a passing trend. Can't we just rock it up tonight? You know, really shake it loose?'

'We can after ten-thirty. We're only supposed to be playing 'til eleven, so it's easy money, man,' Geoff replied as he sat tuning his guitar.

'That's easy for you to say,' Chris interrupted. 'Have you ever tried to play disco funk bass lines all night? No, Geoff, you haven't. All you need to do is play one chord in the rhythm.'

'Will you guys stop bickering? This gig is money in the bank. So, lets enjoy it. Let's get loaded, and let's see what the local talent has to offer, okay?' Bruce said, cleaning his boots for at least the seventh time.

'I'm all for that,' Keith shouted from behind his drums. 'I'm a huge fan of local talent. Give me sixteen-year-old schoolgirls every day of the week. Everyone knows that the chicks dig the drummers.'

'Bullshit. That's only when the drummers are good looking, not fucking trolls like you,' Bruce replied as he opened a small box that he had brought with him.

Inside it there were sandwiches.

'What you got there, man?' Chris asked, sidling over to look in the box. 'Has mommy made you a wittle packed wunch? Bless!'

'Fuck you, man. You know you're just jealous, because your mom's far too wasted to make anything before you leave for a gig,' Bruce retorted in between chews.

'No, man, I get my girlfriend to cook me steak before I gig,' Chris replied, his face flushing ever so slightly.

'Your girlfriend?' Geoff added. 'Your girlfriend? Do you mean that forty-five-year-old, widowed neighbour who you bang every time she comes home loaded?'

'Hey, she's a divorcee, not a widow,' Chris snapped back. 'And, you know... at least I'm having sex.'

'With your hand,' Bruce continued, getting laughs from the others.

Chris began to calm down, realising he was just the butt of the jokes and none of it was personal. 'So, what you got in there, man?' he asked, looking at Bruce's box of delights.

'P B and J,' he replied with a broad grin. 'And yes, there's enough for everyone.'

'Awesome!' Chris shouted, dipping his hand inside.

Bruce slapped it as it went in, and Chris pulled it back quickly, looking at him with hurt eyes. 'What was that for?'

'Have you washed your hands?'

'What?'

'I said, have you washed your hands? I know what a skanky bastard you are. You're not touching my sandwiches until you've washed your hands.'

'Are you fucking serious?' Chris asked, still looking hurt.

'I've been watching you pick your nose, pick your ears, scratch your balls. You're not touching my sandwiches with those flaky fingers. There's just no way!'

'Fuck you, and your P B and fucking J,' Chris hissed.

The rest of the band sniggered at this exchange.

'Hey, Chris?' Bruce shouted, and as the singer turned around, he flung a sandwich towards him. Chris caught it with a grin.

'You're an idiot. You know that?' he said as he bit into the delicious snack.

'Maybe, but at least I don't have flaky fingers.'

'Where the hell is that promoter? He should be here by now. We're due to kick off in an hour,' Keith said, looking at his watch and dipping his hand into Bruce's sandwich box.

'Well, we're all set up and ready to go,' Bruce said.

'Yeah, but we need to be paid, dude!'

'I'm sure he won't let us down. This is the football championship gig. They're not going to fuck this up for anything.'

'I suppose not. It's probably just the weather that's holding him back. Let's get another sound check on the go. We're going to need to be set up and ready as soon as we can,' Keith said, mounting his drum stool and picking up his sticks.

~~~~

Less than two miles away, the promoter was currently sitting behind the wheel of his car, stuck in a flash-flood caused by the incessant rain. The back wheel was half submerged in murky, purplish mud. The promoter was sitting in the driver's seat, shaking his head, and revving the engine, causing the wheels to spin. He was doing this in the vain hope it would gain purchase on something, anything, solid so he wouldn't have to get out of the car and push.

He knew it was futile, the road had turned into a river, and he didn't want to get out into that rain. 'Shit... shit... SHIT ON IT!' he shouted, banging his hand on the steering wheel, marking each curse. 'Why the hell do I take on these shitty backwater gigs?' he yelled at the top of his voice, shouting at the steamed-up windows and the rain pouring outside them. An image of his wife flicked into his head, sitting in their nice warm, dry living room, a glass of wine in her hand, thumbing through the TV guide, looking to find one of those silly creature-feature movies she was fond of, or maybe reading one of those Good Housekeeping magazines she was addicted to.

He wished he was with her right now. Even sitting through one of those stupid movies would be better than this.

With an growl at the back of his throat, he lifted the collar of his raincoat over his ears and unlocked the door. As the light came on inside, it turned all the windows into mirrors, blocking the outside world from his view. He pushed the door open and was hit with a blast of rain that soaked through his coat, wetting his shirt, trousers, even his underwear. *Why the Hell didn't I button this damned coat up?* he cursed, again. 'There's no way on God's Green fucking Earth I'm taking another shitty little town's high school gig, ever again. If the venue isn't right off the fucking freeway...' he vowed, '...they're on their own. Even if the money is good. *This* is not worth fifty bucks!'

The cold rain soaked him and froze him in equal measures. He buttoned up all the buttons in an attempt to stop the freezing water from saturating him more than he already was.

The instant he stepped out, he regretted it. His foot sunk into the deep, muddy river that was flowing freely around him. Filthy brown and purple water ruined his shoes and at least the first few inches of his trousers. His hair was plastered to his head as the rainwater cascaded over his face, dripping from his chin.

Deep down, he felt like he needed to be angry with someone else, someone other than himself, so he cursed his wife. 'I don't know why you don't wear a hat. I always think you look good in a hat!' He mimicked her voice as his anger and frustration swelled.

Once out of the car, and already sopping wet, he looked around for something he could use to help him out of his predicament. The road was deserted, and there was absolutely nothing around. No houses, no public telephones, no other cars, no pedestrians. *Why would there be?* he thought. *I'm the only imbecile out in weather like this.* The only thing he could see, because it was illuminated by the headlights of his car, was an old graveyard surrounded by trees. *Oh fucking brilliant,* he thought as a chill passed through his freezing, wet clothes.

He looked up at the sky, marvelling at the strange purple hue up there. 'Well, I can honestly say I've never been caught in rain from purple clouds before,' he laughed, although he felt very short on humour right now. 'Fucking hick towns, they don't even have normal weather.'

He waded around to the back of the car and looked at the wheel that had been spinning. He could only see the top of it; the bottom half was gone, submerged in the torrent of water that was currently ruining his clothes, and breaking his spirit. He shook his head again, causing spray from his lank hair, as he looked around for something to lever underneath the wheel. He was good with cars and knew a wooden plank or something solid wedged beneath the tyre would give it the purchase it needed to break free. *There's no way I'm walking the rest of the way to that barn, not in this weather.*

He searched his surroundings for something, but it was futile. He seethed as he extended his search into the bushes and the undergrowth at the side of the road.

Still, there was nothing he could use.

39

He rubbed his hands on his lower back, assessing his dire situation. His mouth tightened as his gaze drifted towards the one thing he didn't want to acknowledge. The cemetery. He exhaled deep, from his nose, sending more than a few raindrops into all directions. 'There'll be wood in there, all right,' he mumbled, hating himself for the idea of venturing into a spooky graveyard, alone, in the middle of a storm. Fixing his collar, he made his way along the muddy stream that used to be a road, towards the dark, foreboding cemetery.

Walking with his back to the headlight glare, he continued his search, telling himself that he wasn't scared of the old cemetery at night. His argument held no weight. He was a superstitious person; he always had been. A shiver travelled up his spine, causing the flesh of his arms and chest to break out in goosebumps and his nipples to tighten, painfully.

The shiver had nothing to do with the cold of the night, or the rain, but everything to do with the odd feeling that had just come over him. A feeling like he was being watched. 'Hello,' he shouted. 'Is anyone there?' He hoped there *was* someone there, someone who could help him get the wheel out of the mud so he could get to the barn, pay his clients, *and get the fuck out of this one-horse town.*

The feeling didn't abate, and he spun a full circle, hoping to glimpse whoever was lurking in the shadows, watching him. Something in the periphery vision caught his attention. Something, or someone, was there, he was certain of it, but the glare from the car's headlights, and the spray of the rain, blocked whoever, or whatever, it was from his vision.

'Hey there, friend,' he shouted. 'I'm stuck in the mud. I could really use some help.' Because of the rain streaming down his face, his words came out sounding funny, almost like he was underwater. He wiped his mouth with his soaking sleeve, but it was to no avail. The rain was falling too hard to dry his face. *If there was anyone there, they'd have heard me,* he thought as he continued wading his way towards the old cemetery.

In the light of the headlights, he saw the ground around the tombstones was bubbling and disturbed. He toyed with the idea of rolling his trouser legs up a little to stop them from getting further ruined by the mud, but one look told him, that ship had already sailed. *I'm going to have to throw these trousers away after this little adventure.*

He stepped out of the river of the road, and onto the grass verge. There, he was greeted by a rather comical squelching sound as his foot sunk, deep into the boggy ground. It went way past his ankle. He closed his eyes and clenched his fists. 'Add these shoes to the long list of clothes I'm losing tonight,' he spat as his other leg sunk into the ground almost as deep as the first. He stood, dripping wet, in the torrential rain with both feet submerged in at least three inches of mud, reassessing his life choices. 'If I'd have listened to my dad and become a bus driver like he was, then I wouldn't be in this mess.' Looking like he was offering up a prayer, he thrust his hands into the air and yelled. Once his anger passed, he flapped his arms back to his sides and breathed a wet sigh.

A panic rose when he attempted to lift one of his legs out of the quagmire, to continue his quest for wood, as the foot wouldn't move. Each time he pulled, the mud clung tighter to it, not allowing its prize to slip from its grasp.

'Fuuuuck,' he shouted into the night, as he bent over and grabbed his leg with both hands. With all his strength, he pulled on it. The muddy grip on his limb gave a little, offering him hope in this situation, but it didn't give enough. He closed his eyes, trying to stay calm. He did *not* want to lose his shoes.

Whatever he had seen in his peripheral before, moved. He snapped his head around to see what it could have been. Once again, whatever it was, it was hiding in the glare from the car's headlights. He lifted his hand to shield his eyes from the light. All he could see were several glowing purple dots floating around the trees. He shook his head. 'I don't have time for willow-the-wisps,' he cursed as he returned to the job in hand—freeing himself from the mud.

A noise caught his attention, and once again his head snapped up, this time to listen. It was a cross between the creaking of an old door, a moan, and a growl. 'Shit,' he spat as images of bears, wolves, and hungry, horny dogs flashed through his head. He took a few deep breaths before getting back to work on his legs, in double time.

The noise came again, this time it was accompanied by the movement in the shadows again. Once more he shielded his eyes, but again, he couldn't see anything but floating purple dots. *Are there more of them?* he thought. He stood up straight attempting to focus on the phenomenon. He wracked his brain, trying to remember if he had ever read anything about willow-the-wisps attacking, and killing, people. All he could remember about them was that they were small pockets of swamp gas reacting with the oxygen in the air. In his limited knowledge of the gaseous spectacle, he was, however, certain he'd never heard of any reported sightings of them being able to talk.

'BRRRRRAAAAAAIIINNNNNNSSSSSS!' The half-whisper seemed to come from everywhere. From the trees, from the mud, from the night itself.

'Brains,' he scoffed. 'Fucking crazy imagination!'

'BRRRRRAAAAAAIIINNNNNNSSSSSS!'

This time, it wasn't a whisper.

The goosebumps were back, this time they were all over his body, not just his arms and chest. He hadn't mis-heard it, of this, he was sure. The single, drawn out hiss was one hundred percent a word, and it was one hundred percent the word *brains!*

He laughed at the absurdity of this situation. Here he was, stuck in the mud, in a cemetery, in the middle of a storm, with an aggressive willow-the-wisp advancing upon him that wanted to eat his brains.

'Maybe I should write a book,' he laughed to himself. 'That's it. When I get home, I'm going to quit this crappy agent job, buy myself a typewriter, and write the shit out of a new book.'

Lost in his new train of thought, the promoter failed to notice, what he had originally thought of as a willow-the-wisp was, uncharacteristically for that particular phenomenon, getting closer rather than further away.

'A stupid man, who's made stupid choices in life, gets his stupid car stuck in some stupid mud in a stupid hick town in the middle of fucking stupid nowhere. That should do it,' he laughed, tugged at his legs, trying his best to get out of the absurd situation he had found himself in.

'BRRRRRAAAAAAIIINNNNNNSSSSSS!'

He stopped pulling for a moment, and stood up again, a little too fast this time, and his head began to swim. He knew what he'd heard. He knew it wasn't the wind whistling through the trees. He knew it wasn't the rain pouring and splashing into puddles. He knew it wasn't birds in the trees, sheltering from the storm.

Come to think of it, he thought, *why is there absolutely no other sounds other than the rain and whatever it is making the 'brains' noise?*

'BRRRRRAAAAAAIIINNNNNNSSSSSS!'

He scanned for the source of the sound, once again raising his hand to block out the glaring light from the headlights of his car. The first thing he noticed was that the purple lights were closer.

A lot closer.

He then noticed they were attached to something, or somethings, plural. He noticed that for every two lights, there seemed to be a head they were set in. *Almost like...*

EYES!

Oh shit, they're eyes, attached to heads, attached to bodies. His brain, for the first time registering that he was petrified, jumped to the logical conclusion that his rational mind couldn't be right.

Only, it was. He suddenly found himself surrounded by... *by what?* he asked himself. *Come on brain, if you're so fucking clever, answer me that. By what?*

Lumbering out of the darkness of the graveyard and into the stark light, came a...

ANSWER ME! he shouted at himself in his own head. He was far too scared to shout out loud. *What could they possibly be?*

He concluded they were men. Or maybe women. Either way, they were human, or had *been* human, once. Maybe a long, long time ago.

The lead thing had hair. Not a lot of it, but there were bits, strands, hanging here and there. It looked long and perhaps had once been black. *Or maybe that's just the rain,* he thought, trying to justify what he was seeing. As it got closer, he saw that the eyes were not eyes at all. They were glowing, raging fires set within in two purple whirlpools. Everything else about it looked dead, rotten, and decrepit. Its clothes ripped, dirty, and outdated, its limbs moved in a way that denoted stiffness. Its jaw however, looked alive, hungry, and dangerous.

'BRRRRRAAAAAAIIINNNNNNSSSSSS!'

Panic set in. Deep panic.

His brain didn't want to comprehend what he was seeing and began to rebel, instilling absurd song lyrics into his psyche. The Carpenters, *I fucking hate The Carpenters,* he thought. *Why is "Top of the World" running through my head? Am I still in my book?* He then realised that if he was, he wasn't the strong hero who strides through the mud to slay the vile creatures surrounding him. He was most definitely the victim who soiled himself as the creatures surrounded him.

'BRRRRRAAAAAAIIINNNNNNSSSSSS!'

This was the very last word he heard as a sentient human being.

Cold, strong, hands gripped him, and he felt stinking, cold breath on his neck. As the intense pain began, his eyes rolled towards the back of his head and the whole world went black.

~~~~

The blackout was a mercy, but only a small one. No-one would have wanted to write a book about a lowly band promoter with his two feet stuck in mud, being torn apart by undead ghouls in a dark graveyard in the middle of a bizarre purple rainstorm. It was not the glorious ending that literary heroes in tales of bravado and derring-do had.

Unfortunately for this pissed off band promoter, it turned out he was the first victim in his cheap, pulp horror novel.

11.

THE PARTY WAS already in full swing as the boys made their way into the barn. One of the teachers, Mr Turnbull, who was overseeing the welcoming committee, was there to greet them. 'Boys,' he purred, pushing his thick glasses up onto the bridge of his nose. He looked at his watch. 'You're just in time. I'm going to need you to go around the back and get changed. When the girls arrive, we'll start the show. They'll march on, start the proceedings, then you guys enter carrying the cup. The others from the team are already here, so if you'd pop into the back before anyone sees you, that would be fantastic.'

'Come on, men, it's our night of glory,' Jason said, addressing his friends. He opened his coat, flashing the bottle of booze that was languishing inside.

Razor looked at it and grinned, before opening his own coat, flashing a similar bottle. 'Looks like we're going to have ourselves a party after all.' Hank slapped him five as they followed the teacher into a room around the back of the stage area.

The muffled sounds of the band playing some funky disco tunes in the main hall filtered in. 'That band can really wail,' Brad said, moving along to the grinding rhythm.

'Yes, they are rather good, I'd say. Quite... what's the word? Flunky?' Mr Turnbull said, indicating the door to the changing room.

'Yeah, that's exactly the word I'd use, Mr Turnbull. They're extremely flunky,' Jason said, laughing. The others joined in.

'Well, it took a little bit of persuading to get them to begin, as their promoter hasn't showed up with their money. We explained he's probably running a little late due to the weather. Which is probably the same thing that's happening to the girls. They should have been here before you,' the teacher explained opening the door for them.

'The girls aren't here yet?' Jason asked.

'Not yet, but I believe they shouldn't be long.'

Jason's face fell. Razor nudged him, and he turned to see a grin spreading over his friend's face.

'Don't worry,' he whispered. 'She'll be here.'

All the other members of the football team were already inside, and a cheer rang out for the entrance of their star quarterback. In the centre of the room, food had been laid out on a table, and there was a large punchbowl too. As the greetings and low-five hand slaps finished, Mr Turnbull turned to leave. 'You just need to stay in here until we announce you. Shouldn't be any longer than half an hour or so. Once the girls arrive, we'll get them on to lead the cheering, and then it's your turn. Is everyone OK with that?'

'I think we can live with this, Mr Turnbull,' Razor said, making his way to the punchbowl, reaching into his coat for the bottle of booze.

'That's just fruit punch, obviously,' Mr Turnbull explained as he exited the door. 'I'll come back and check on you shortly. Don't get into any trouble now!'

'We won't,' Jason replied as he took out his bottle. 'We'll just sit here and listen to the flunky beats of the band.' He opened the lid of the bottle, and to many shouts of encouragement, he poured the whole contents into the bowl, bringing the level up to the top. 'Gentlemen,' he said, addressing the team assembled before him. 'Tonight, we are the returning heroes. And *as* heroes, we drink to celebrate the defeat of our enemies.'

'Did anyone else think that Old Turnbull seemed in a hurry to get away?' Hank asked as he dipped his plastic cup into the mixture.

'Man, what rock have you been under?' Kevin asked. 'He's Wellborn's latest squeeze. Didn't you know?'

Hank shook his head as he, too, dipped his cup. 'I thought she'd already been through the whole school.'

'Not yet, obviously,' Jason said as he held up his dripping plastic cup. As was the tradition, the quarterback had to knock back his drink before the others, which he did to many more whoops, low-fives, and cheers. Once he put the cup upside down on his head, the rest of the team dipped their cups deep into the fiery liquid before drinking even deeper.

~~~~

In the hall, the band was well into their first set. The crowd had all turned up at pretty much the same time, so they had decided, upon a promise from Mr Turnbull that their fee would be paid from the entertainment committee's funds if the promoter didn't turn up, to begin their set. It was shaping up to be a successful night. Bruce and Geoff were happy that the high school kids looked mostly on the legal side of sixteen and that the chaperones of the younger ones looked to be well over the legal age limit.

'I don't care,' Keith had announced before they had taken to the stage. He had been looking around and getting (and giving) the eye from several of the girls in the room. 'It's like I've always said, they're old enough when they've left school!'

'When have you ever said that?' Geoff questioned him between songs.

'At half past three!' Keith replied with a wink.

Geoff shook his head and stepped a little away from the decadent drummer. 'You, my friend, are a dirty old goat, and you deserve to have daughters when you're older. That would be God paying you back for a life of debauchery.'

'Yeah, like you don't agree with me, you perv,' Keith laughed, as he got himself comfortable behind the drumkit.

'I might,' he said, returning the wink at his friend. 'But I don't go around shouting it from the rooftops like you.'

Keith laughed again. He looked around for the nod that said everyone was ready to move onto the next song. Once he had confirmation, he banged his sticks together four times, and they kicked into a groovy disco beat that got everyone up onto the dance floor almost immediately.

12.

OLDMAN WAS IN the kitchen; he was seldom anywhere else. The apron he was wearing used to be pristine white but was now more than just a little beige. The pink frilly trim to the cotton could have been an analogy for his life; it had started off vibrant but was now faded and frayed. He was standing by the stove stirring a large pot with a wooden spoon. Steam was flowing from the lid. He leaned over it and sniffed. He rolled his eyes, smiled, and nodded. The stew was nearly ready. He placed the spoon on the counter, then took another, smaller spoon out of the drawer. He dipped this one into the mixture and tasted the sauce. He hummed to himself. 'Oh yes!' he proclaimed. 'Perfect.'

'What did you say, honey?' Oldgirl asked as she looked up from the engine, she was stripping on the kitchen table.

'Nothing, dear,' he replied. 'I was just tasting the stew. It's delicious.'

'Oh, good,' she replied, returning her attention to her job at hand. 'I'm starving. Working them fields all day sure does give a gal an appetite.'

'I really wish you wouldn't do that on the kitchen table. We have to eat there,' he moaned, putting the glass lid back on top of the pot.

'I know, I'm sorry, honey, but where else am I going to do it?'

'Erm, I don't know,' he sighed. 'How about the garage, where you're supposed to do it?'

'In this weather? Have you seen that rain? It's frigging purple! You wouldn't want me getting caught in the garage in a purple storm, would you?' she asked with a sly grin that only caused more wrinkles to appear on her already abundantly wrinkled face.

He rolled his eyes, tutted, and turned back to his stew.

She grinned as she resumed stripping the engine.

'It *is* some storm out there,' he said, more to make conversation than anything else. 'I haven't seen rain like that for years. In any case, I don't think I've *ever* seen it purple. I hope the party in the barn isn't affected.'

'If I know teenagers, and I do, then even the dead rising from their graves wouldn't stop them from a good party,' she answered as she selected a wrench from the oily toolbox languishing on the table next to the filthy parts. 'When will that dinner be ready, husband? I could eat a hobo's foot right about now.'

Oldman removed the lid again and took another sniff, he then dipped the small spoon again. He smacked his lips tighter as he tasted it. 'Momentarily, my sweetness,' he replied. 'I think this could be my best one to date. Just the thing on a night like this.'

As he went to the cupboard to get the bowls, he glanced out of the window, over towards the fields. Something caught his eye. He leaned in, blocking the light inside the house to see what he thought he saw clearly.

There were two glowing pinpricks of purple light hovering around outside. On closer look, he realised there were more than two, in fact there was a whole bunch of them. They were moving up the path, towards their house.

He stepped away from the window and shook his head. *Did I just see that?* he thought before going back to have another look.

'What are you looking at out there, you cranky old bird?' Oldgirl cackled from behind her engine.

'I don't know,' he replied, still looking out of the window. The purple lights were closer. Through the rain and the streaks on the window, he couldn't make out how they were floating. He thought maybe they were local kids joking about, or maybe it was some of the revellers from the party in the barn, less than a mile in the other direction. He shook his head; *how could they be doing that?* He dismissed the phenomenon and continued to serve the stew into the bowls.

'I just saw the damnedest thing,' he muttered as he put the bowls of steaming supper on the table between the oily engine parts.

'Yeah?' Oldgirl asked, pushing aside the engine block, and grabbing a spoon.

He knew she had no real interest in what he had just said, but he pressed on regardless. 'Yeah. I think I just saw a swarm of fireflies, or at least I think they were fireflies. Are fireflies purple?'

'Hm?' Oldgirl asked as she spooned a large helping of the stew into her mouth.

'Are fireflies purple?' he asked again.

She shook her head. 'Nope, yellow. Always yellow,' she answered slurping more stew.

'Well then, I've got no idea what it was I just saw, but they were swarming towards the house,' he said, sitting down at the table and grabbing his spoon. As he took a heap of the meal, he smacked his lips together. 'Now that is what I call a nice stew.'

'It's OK,' Oldgirl replied taking another spoonful.

'Mmmmmmmmmeeeeeeerrrrrrrrr!'

'What?' she asked, looking up from her meal.

'I said, that's a nice stew,' he repeated, taking another spoonful. She nodded.

'Mmmmmmmmmeeeeeeerrrrrrrrr!'

'What?' she asked again, looking up at her husband, who had his spoon sticking out of his mouth.

'Huh?' he asked, unable to articulate.

'Will you stop making noises? It's annoying,' she snapped.

'I'm not making any noises,' he protested, removing the spoon from his mouth.

She shook her head and swallowed another mouthful.

'Mmmmmmmmmeeeeeeerrrrrrrrr!'

Oldgirl slammed her spoon on the table, making the engine parts rattle with the force of the impact. 'I said stop it, goddammit!' she shouted, bits of meat and potato flew from her mouth as she spat the words.

'I'm not doing anything, woman,' Oldman shouted back, spraying his own volume of stew.

'Mmmmmmmmmeeeeeeerrrrrrrrr!'

They stopped fighting and looked at each other.

'Did you hear that?' Oldman asked, swallowing the mouthful of dinner that was languishing inside his mouth.

Oldgirl's eyes moved from left to right, checking out the room. 'I heard something,' she whispered.

They both pushed their bowls aside and stood. Both sets of eyes were drawn towards the kitchen window. The glass was decorated in silvery spots where the light reflected the rain drops outside. Mixed in with the silver were several glowing purple lights.

'There they are,' he shouted excitedly. 'I told you. Purple fireflies.' He pointed towards the window where the lights were burning like the strangest fire either of them had ever seen. 'Look, can you see them?'

She was looking where Oldman was pointing. She was marvelling at the dozen or more dancing purple flames at the window.

'I told you there were purple fireflies,' he shouted, in a high pitched, excited voice. 'I told you, I told you.' He was chanting now, pointing at the lights through the window.

Oldgirl narrowed her eyes as she moved closer.

A shadowy something shifted in the darkness, and the lights moved with it.

'Oldman,' she whispered.

He heard the waver in her voice and didn't like it.

'I don't think they're fireflies,' she finished, moving away from the window.

'What? Are you stupid, woman? Of course they're fireflies. What else could they...'

The noise of the glass shattering drowned out what remained of his sentence. They were both forced backwards by the violence of the explosion that took them by surprise, covering them in dangerous slivers of broken glass.

'What in tarnation?' Oldgirl shouted as she fell away from the exploding window. As she dropped, she reached out and grabbed the straps of her husband's apron, dragging him down on top of her.

He landed on his backside on the hard kitchen floor. Ignoring the pain in his hands, and buttocks, where the glass sliced him, he was up in a flash. Slivers of glass tore his exposed flesh as he scurried along the floor on all fours, leaving behind him a trail of blood. Somehow, his old boots gained traction on the slippery floor, and he managed to scramble into an upright position. Without even a glance at what had caused the explosion, he made it to the sink and opened the cupboard door beneath.

He could hear the tinkling of the glass and the moan of his wife as she lay on the floor covered in the sharp splinters. She was attempting to get up. There was another noise too, a familiar noise, one that he recognised from the dinner table not two minutes earlier.

'Mmmmmmmmmeeeeeeerrrrrrrrr!'

Did I hear that right? he thought as he rummaged through the cupboard. *I could have sworn it said...*

'BRRRRRAAAAAAIIINNNNNNSSSSSS!'

A shiver ran down his back at the thought of the drawn-out word, and the connotations it brought to their situation. He continued searching beneath the sink until he found what he was looking for. He stood up and swung around, just in time to see Oldgirl getting herself up from the glass strewn floor and dusting herself off. *Thank God she's OK!*

Then, he saw them.

They weren't fireflies after all.

They were bigger ... and much scarier.

One of them had pushed its head through the window; *probably what smashed it, to be fair,* he thought as he held on tightly to the large, bright yellow can of insect repellent retrieved from the cupboard. The ugly face, much uglier than his was, and that was ugly, was now looking at him gnashing its teeth together. It was of indeterminate gender. It was bald with dirty, mottled skin. What he had thought of as lovely purple fireflies turned out to be ghastly balls of flame blazing in the dark holes that had once housed eyeballs.

It was using its skeletal arms to prize itself in through the window.

'BRRRRRAAAAAAIIINNNNNNSSSSSS!'

The hiss came from the thing hanging in the window. He didn't know if it was saying the word 'brains' or if it only sounded like it was, either way, he didn't care. He wanted that thing far away from him, from his wife, and from his house, preferably in that order.

Another two monsters had turned up to the party and were attempting to climb in through the window. The purple wildfire of their eyes was concentrated on the stricken woman who was still trying to brush glass from her overalls.

'Get out! Get out, spawn of Hell...' he screamed.

The scream didn't have the effect he desired. All he'd managed to do was catch the attention of two others who were outside, vying to get in.

'BRRRRRAAAAAAIIINNNNNNNSSSSSS!' they hissed as thin, decaying arms swiped at him.

Another noise from behind alerted him, and he whipped around to see what it was. To his horror, there were two more purple lights glowing through the small window above the kitchen door that led into the yard.

'Get them, you dullard,' came a shout he recognised. As he snapped his head back towards the main window, he saw that two of the things were inside and were already clambering over his wife. He raised the can of insect spray, ready to attack.

He hesitated. It was for just a single, solitary moment. *Hmm,* he thought. *I wonder what life would be like without her…*

Instantly, he was transformed from the kitchen in the drab, old cottage, to find himself in a rather nice lounge. He was sat at a table behind a tall cake stand that was brimming with delightfully coloured confectionaries. There was a china teapot before him, with two cups. He looked up from the delicious spread to see the face of…

… his wife, being torn apart by two hideous, rotting beasts!

He looked at the yellow can of insect repellent; it was as good a weapon as anything else.

An unholy roar erupted from somewhere. It was a moment later, and much to his surprise, that he realised it was coming from him. He used the bravado the roar brought to rush at the beasts, who now had his screaming wife pinned to the floor while they fought over which one of them were going to eat her first.

'Have some of this, you bastards,' he shouted, running at them, the tips of his fingers turning white as he pressed the nozzle of the can.

The white spray arched into the air. The stream found its targets and began to foam in the faces of the beasts. Their grunts and growls changed, morphing into vile, bloodcurdling screams as they released Oldgirl, unceremoniously dropping her onto the hard kitchen tiles. As one, they began to scratch violently at their faces.

Battered and bloody, Oldgirl managed to scurry away using her elbows and knees. Oldman stopped spraying and reached out a hand to pull his wife out of the grasp of the things. As he dragged her to safety, he noticed at least two open wounds in her skin where she had been bitten. Both wounds looked to have a little of the purple fire within the blood that was spilling from them. He blinked his eyes to clear them of tears and sweat, hoping his brain had been playing tricks on him.

It hadn't!

There *was* a purple tinge to her blood.

'What are you gawping at, idiot? Get them things out of our house,' she spat.

That was his cue to start spraying again.

This time, his aim wasn't as true as the first time. The white spray arched high into the air but missed its marks, by a long shot.

Oldgirl's gaze was on the door. More of the glowing purple lights were now peering through the window at the top. She looked over at her husband, currently battling two animated skeletons with the large yellow can of insect repellent, then looked out of the broken window at the multitude of purple lights outside. She dived, not very gracefully, underneath the dining table that still had their stew cooling in the bowls above. The instant she was safe underneath, two loud bangs reported around the room as the wood of the door began to rattle against its frame.

The monsters outside seemed rather anxious to get inside.

Sparing a glance towards her husband, she yanked at the tablecloth, attempting to pull it down over her head.

It wouldn't come. It was lodged beneath the heavy, partially stripped engine on the top of the table. Raging with herself for not heeding her husband's advice, she tugged on it again. It ripped, and the force of her effort knocked her onto the floor. As her head connected with the hard kitchen tiles, there was an almighty crack, and the tablecloth covered her head.

Oldman wasn't doing much better in his battle with the undead things that had invaded their house. He had advanced on the squealing monsters, still spraying, and still missing them, with the insect repellent. In his false bravado, he hadn't been prepared for the worst thing that could have happened—something that set his fight against the marauding hoard attacking his home back, considerably.

He slipped on the discharged foam and fell, almost comically, onto his back.

He fell like a character in an old black and white comedy, one where the thin, dopey type would inadvertently leave a banana skin on the floor, and the big, bossy type, who was always the fall guy for the thin guy's misgivings, would step on it. He flew into the air and landed in an almost perfect horizontal position.

As he fell, the thick, white spray from his can changed direction, it was now spraying onto his face and into his eyes.

The stinging was unmerciful. It felt like someone had emptied a box of hot pins into his face and was rubbing them in.

He tried to scream, but the fall had knocked the wind out of him, and the sour poison from the can was trickling into his mouth. All he managed to issue was a pathetic mewling, gurgle.

The two marauding *things* recovered quickly from their attack and were joined by another two who had been outside, but had now made it inside. If either Oldman, or Oldgirl, had been able to see, they would have realised there had been very little hope for them in this battle from the beginning, as a multitude of purple lights began to stream into the kitchen from the smashed window.

From somewhere outside the pain from his eyes and his back, Oldman could hear a banging noise.

One... two... three...

It was followed by a CRASH!

It sounded like the kitchen door had been forced open.

It had.

Four more monsters fell over each other, into the small, rustic kitchen, all of them eager to get at the promised meal inside.

Oldgirl had roused from her knock and was holding the tablecloth tight over her head. Oldman was struggling to get up while dealing with the pain of the insect repellent in his eyes.

'BRRRRRAAAAAAIIINNNNNNSSSSSS!'

Both heard the word as it filled the room. Oldman reached out a bloodied hand, searching for the rough hand of his wife. Oldgirl did the same. By some cosmic miracle, their hands met, they gripped each other tight, as they resigned themselves to their hideous fate.

'BRRRRRAAAAAAIIINNNNNNSSSSSS!'

They would never get to finish the best stew that Oldman had ever made, as the room was soon redecorated in a dark, fresh crimson.

~~~~

If the rain hadn't been hammering so hard from the strange, coloured sky, the bloodcurdlingly wet screams that tore from the farmhouse might have been heard as far across the fields as the barn, where the party was currently in full swing. It most definitely would have been heard on Cemetery Road, parallel to the graveyard, where a certain Oldsmobile filled with six excited, and anxious, cheerleaders was currently racing along the treacherously muddy roads, en-route to the aforementioned barn to join said party.

But, as it was, all the car's passengers could hear above the racket made by the old car's engine, and the rumpus made by the band currently giving their all from the radio, was the relentless pounding of the rain as it continued to fall in torrents from the thick, purple clouds.

13.

'WE'RE GOING TO be late,' Birdie worried, looking out the passenger window of the Oldsmobile as it raced along Cemetery Road. 'The boys aren't going to be happy about this.'

What looked like a hundred pompoms were crammed in-between the six girls squeezed almost on top of each other as Pamela sped along the treacherous back roads, her foot almost to the metal. Wave after wave of muddy water crashed over the grass verges with each puddle they splashed through.

'Well, if you hadn't needed to fix your hair a thousand times, we would have been fine,' Suzi snapped as she gazed out of the window she was pushed up against. Her eyes were drawn upwards, towards the purple clouds hanging low in the sky.

'My new 'do just wasn't cutting it. I need to look my best. You of all people should know that,' Birdie argued.

'But you could see the weather, and you knew we were already late,' Pamela chirped in from the driver's seat as she flicked the strands of a pompom out from underneath her nose.

'Listen, we're on our way, we're all looking fine, and it's gonna be a blast. Anyway, it's fashionable to turn up late to parties. Everyone will be watching out for us as we strut in shaking what our mommas gave us,' Wendy added, putting a smile on all the girls' faces.

'And when we do that routine, Je-sus, that's going to blow some minds,' Betty added.

'It's so fucking hot. It's gonna start some trouser movements for sure,' Suzi added to the screams of encouragement from the rest of the girls. 'There may even be some explosions,' she continued with a grin.

'Like you even need that,' Wendy shouted over the screaming. 'Jason's got a permanent boner just *thinking* about you, you big sexy afro-bitch!' She rubbed her hand into her friend's large mane.

'Don't mess with the 'fro, sister,' she laughed, reaching up to grab the hand making its way through her hair.

As she did, the car swerved on the wet road.

The girls screamed as Pamela fought with the steering wheel to keep control of the overly laden vehicle. Luckily, due to the inclement weather, there were nothing else on the road, otherwise they might have been in trouble. Eventually, she got all four wheels to point in the same direction, and the car corrected itself.

'Shit,' Suzi shouted once they had straightened out. 'Pam, will you quit auditioning for a cheesy cop show?'

'Sorry, baby,' she replied. 'It's just so wet out there.'

'I know, but the way you're driving, it's going to be wet in here too. I nearly peed my panties.' Suzi breathed deeply as she rubbed her hand through the black velvet goodness of her hair.

Pamela looked at the clock on the dash. 'I reckon we've got about ten minutes before they start thinking about going on without us.'

'Going on with nobody leading the cheering? Never going to happen,' Wendy snapped, looking out the window at the rain beating against it. 'Surely, they'll wait for us.'

'They'll wait,' Betty added. 'No-one's there to look at the boys in their football jerseys. They're all waiting for our swagger and short skirts,' she laughed, pulling her cheerleader jersey tight over her ample chest.

The rest of the car laughed along with her.

'We're not going to be late anyway,' Suzi said as she looked out the front windshield. 'The barn's just up this road.'

As she pointed towards the lights ahead of them, something lurched into the road.

Suzi screamed.

Whatever it had been, it had crossed in a hurry, then disappeared into the bushes on the other side.

Suzi's scream panicked Pamela, who in turn oversteered the car again. As the rubber of the tyres turned in tandem with the wheel, the water, and the mud underneath them, caused them to lose purchase on the soggy road, sending the car into a headlong skid.

Unfortunately, Pamela wasn't savvy in the ways of the road, and she fought the wheel, trying to turn against the skid. This just caused the vehicle to fishtail. The backend slid in the opposite direction, and they began to spin.

Everyone in the car was screaming.

All of them, all at the same time.

The Oldsmobile was out of control. As it spun, and the girls spun with it, it began to rock. When it rocked, it began to tip. Soon, there were only two tyres contacting what remained of the road. And both of them were ready to give up.

It wasn't long before they did.

The car flipped in the air and came to a standstill on its roof.

The water cascading along the road, in a makeshift river, streamed into the vehicle, soaking everyone inside. The screaming had stopped, as had the high-pitched protestations of the metal chassis. The only sounds that could be heard was the gentle tinkle of running water along the road, coupled with the pounding of the rain on the upside-down vehicle.

The passenger side door popped open. It was quickly followed by one of the rear ones, then the other front one. Before long, all four doors were wide open.

Six bruised, beaten, muddy, and badly shaken girls rolled out. None of them said a word. They all just lay on the swampy road, as silent as the graveyard next to them.

Suzi, Pamela, Betty, Birdie, Wendy, and Nicky crawled away from the crash site and lay, on their backs, in a circle. Their dirty faces looked up to the sky. Their once pristine and pressed cheerleader outfits were ruined as brown, muddy water rushed over them. Their immaculately coiffured hair and intricate makeup was also ruined.

The six of them lay, silently staring up at the shifting, swirling, tumultuous, purple clouds.

Whether by coincidence or by design, each of their limbs were touching the girl next to them, forming an unbroken circle.

Something strange happened then.

The clouds parted. A small opening allowed a flash of dark blue evening twilight sky in the girls' zenith to present itself. A whirlwind of purple formed within the opening, and streaks of lightning zapped through the clouds towards it, briefly illuminating the scene below.

The lightning bolts didn't dissipate once they had reached the clearing, however. Instead, they began to merge within the maelstrom, spiralling within the clouds, creating a vortex. The light began to spin, faster and faster, until the whole clearing was a ball of revolving light.

This light reflected from each of the girls' eyes as they stared, unblinking, at the spectacle above them.

No-one thought to speak. There was nothing to say anyway.

Without warning, a brilliant, mauve flare streaked from the turmoil. It was similar in appearance to the original fork of lightning that hit the graveyard earlier that afternoon. The purple prong cast from the sky with an unprecedented violence. It crashed to the ground, causing an explosion, the epicentre of which happened to be within the circle the girls had formed. The water bubbling around them was instantly illuminated. The mud they were lying in began to bubble and boil. An eruption of sludge swelled around the circle of cheerleaders, swallowing them, all sucking them down; burying them alive.

As they vanished beneath the violent, violet phenomenon, not one of them moved; not even to close their eyes.

~~~~

Within a few moments, the incident was over. The lightning had dissipated, and the mud was once again the regular, dirty brown that it should always have been. The only evidence of the accident the cheerleaders had found themselves in was an overturned Oldsmobile, lying discarded on the edge of the road, one of its wheels still revolving.

In the fields opposite, things were lurking in the undergrowth. Things that shouldn't have existed.

They were the undead. The stinking, rotten, unnaturally animated cadavers of past residents of the small town of Kearney. Their glowing, purple eyes had witnessed the accident. Whatever intelligence was acting within them had informed them that their all-time favourite snack, brains, was now being served on the road like the world's worst buffet, just waiting for them to help themselves.

But the lightning had scared them away.

Something about it had triggered whatever basic, instinctive intelligence they possessed, informed them that whatever had just happened, it would serve them best to steer clear of it. There were better, richer, easier rewards to be had in the large structure further down the road. The one with the awful noises coming from it.

So, as a herd, they ignored the overturned vehicle, and marched onwards, towards lunch.

14.

'OK, WE'RE A little concerned about the girls. They're either uncharacteristically late, or just not coming. We're going to have to do the presentation without them,' Mr Turnbull announced as he stood in the doorway of the changing room at the back of the stage.

'We can't go on without them,' Razor protested, looking out of the back window towards the now packed parking lot. The rain was still pouring, but he could see there were no other lights on the oncoming road, lights that might have indicated the girls were turning up.

'We're going to have to,' Turnbull continued. 'Those kids out there aren't going to hang around for long waiting to cheer you on. They want to party. The band is kicking up a storm.'

'There's no way the girls are going to miss this,' Jason protested looking at his watch. 'There must be something wrong. Has anyone telephoned their houses to see if they've turned up there?' He knew Mr Turnbull was right. They were going to have to go out and parade the cup and do it soon. It was what everyone was here tonight to see, after all.

'There's a telephone installed in the office, and we tried, but it seems that the storm has taken down some of the lines in the area. I'm going to send Ms Wellborn out to Suzi Afron's house to see if they've heard anything from her, or her friends. In the meantime, we need to get you guys out on the stage. We need to show off that cup.'

'Yeah, come on, let's do it,' Brad shouted. 'Then we can get loaded on that punch.'

Mr Turnbull looked at him, cocking his head to one side.

'Erm…' Brad continued. 'You know. Because it's full to the brim with vitamins and stuff,' he replied, flinging his arms out from his chest as if he were performing an exercise. 'You know how us athletes love our vitamins,' he concluded.

Mr Turnbull's eyebrows narrowed as he looked at the boy. He then shook his head and turned to leave. 'I'm going to announce you in ten minutes. All you need to do is get on the stage, show the cup around, and then get off again when the applause dies down.'

'But what about the girls?' Brad asked again.

'Ms Wellborn will find them, don't you worry about that. Ten minutes, gentlemen, and do me a huge favour…'

The whole of the football team looked at him.

'No profanity. You may think pulling a mooner is the height of sophistication, but please be aware, it's all been done before.'

'I wonder if anyone has ever pulled a *front* mooner?' Rob asked, nudging Jason with a grin.

Jason nodded and smiled, but his thoughts were somewhere else. *The girls would* never *miss this,* he thought.

~~~~

Ms Wellborn was in her late thirties. She was a spinster and liked that situation very much. She loved being single, it gave her all the space she needed to pursue her life passions without the need to justify herself to any bothering spouse.

And she had many passions to pursue.

She was a very passionate woman!

Currently, her passion was Mr Turnbull, and, unknown to Mrs Turnbull, or indeed any other members of the faculty, she was his passion too. Over the years of being the Kearney High School librarian, she had pretty much worked her way through the whole of the male faculty, and a sizeable chunk of the females too. As a woman, she had needs, and she would not allow anything to interfere with her tending to them.

When Mr Turnbull had asked her to go and look for the missing cheerleaders, she understood his meaning completely. He meant *meet me on Cemetery Road*, their usual tryst location.

'If you don't find them, I'll join in the search,' he'd added, giving her a small wink, and a nod, that told her the true nature of his request.

She was currently driving out of the parking area with one hand on the wheel while the other, rather expertly, was removing her bra from beneath her blouse.

~~~~

'Ladies and gentlemen, please put your hands together for the nineteen seventy-seven District Champions football team. Let me hear you roar for... The Lions!' Mr Turnbull announced as the team made their way between the band members, onto the stage.

Jason appeared from the side, holding a large silver cup above his head. This caused the crowd to break into a spontaneous rapture. Shouts of 'Li-Ons, Li-Ons, Li-Ons,' could be heard from everywhere.

The calls and the chants continued as the other members of the team walked out, all of them waving and vying to hold, and kiss, the cup.

'Where's the cheerleaders?' came a shout from the crowd.

'Bring on the cheerleaders,' came another.

Mr Turnbull's face fell. He raised his hands in the air, and the crowd calmed a little, enough for him to be heard. He stepped up to the singer's microphone, and the loud high-pitched whine from the speakers quietened the audience quicker that he had been able to. 'Ladies and gentlemen, boys and girls, there seems to be a bit of an issue with the cheerleaders,' he announced. 'They are running a little late. We've sent Ms Wellborn out to find them.' He looked at his watch and frowned, a little too theatrically. 'Actually, she's been gone for a small while herself. I might have to send a search party out for the search party.' He was the only one who laughed at this joke. 'So, I'll go and see if I can find her...'

This caused a few raised eyebrows from kids in the audience; most of them knew what Ms Wellborn was like, and they knew exactly where Mr Turnbull was going to look for her.

Cemetery Road!

There were more than a few whistles and *woos* from the kids. The band members smiled also.

Mr Turnbull's face flushed bright red. He cleared his throat and pulled at the collar of his shirt. 'I, erm, shouldn't be too long.'

'I bet you won't,' came a shout from somewhere in the room.

As the crowd laughed at the well times hackle, Mr Turnbull's face flushed an even deeper red and he fixed his glasses back up to the top of his nose. 'Anyway, I'll just go and see if I can find her. Mr Grange will be in charge in my absence. If there's anything you need, then see him. OK? Right, I'll see you all very soon.' And with that, he exited the stage, in something of a flurry, and was out of the main doors in a flash, rushing into the rain without even putting his coat on.

~~~~

Ms Wellborn, despite the weather, made it to Cemetery Road unscathed and parked in her regular spot. It was well secluded, away from the road and perfectly camouflaged from any prying eyes by the thick trees and bushes all around.

As she pulled into the spot she had been frequenting since she had been in high school, she put the car into park and killed the engine. A sly smile spread across her face in anticipation of the delights Mr Turnbull would be imparting upon her very soon. She reached underneath her long, conservative skirt and began to un-hook her garters. Next, she slid out of her panties. She didn't want to remove the sheer stockings as Mr Turnbull rather enjoyed them.

Despite of the rain, she let her window down a little, and she hung the bright pink underwear out of the window before closing it again, allowing them to blow in the wind. It was an indication, a flag, to her current beau, letting him know that she was ready, willing, and waiting for his attentions.

~~~~

Mr Turnbull was speeding down the muddy road, far too fast than was safe for the conditions. The wipers were working double-time on his windscreen—if he could, he would have turned them up even faster. He leaned forward and wiped at the window, hoping to remove some of the condensation built up by the warmth within the car.

There was an air of excitement and expectation about him. He knew exactly where he would find Ms Wellborn, and he knew exactly what delights she was about to bestow on him. *Best of both worlds,* he thought. *Get away from those horrible kids—all they think about is sex, sex, sex—and get to spend some sweet quality time with the delectable Ms Wellborn.* The duality of this thought was lost within the powerful, lustful feelings, and cravings, currently tickling his belly, and parts even lower.

More than once, he felt the tires swerving to the left and to the right as the incessant rain continued to teem from the sky, but none of this bothered him. He knew it would be both warm and dry in her car, and he knew the heat, that would be coming from both of their bodies, would fend off any chills that might come their way.

The fan was blowing full on the windows, and it really should have been defogging them better, but it wasn't. As soon as he wiped the mist away, it was already beginning to fog back up again.

As he skidded onto Cemetery Road, wiping the condensation built up from his last wipe, something staggered in front of the car.

'Shit!' he screamed as he oversteered the wheel to avoid hitting whatever it was. Now, Mr Turnbull had been driving for considerably more years than Pamela, who had been driving the Oldsmobile, and he knew all about turning *into* a skid to avoid losing control. So, dutifully, he performed the manoeuvre admirably. Unfortunately for him, Cemetery Road was not the widest of roads, and his car lurched as it hit a ditch that ran along the verge before shuddering to a stop.

'Fuck, fuck… FUCK!' he shouted, hitting the steering wheel with his fists, inadvertently setting off the horn.

~~~~

Ms Wellborn could hear a car horn blaring from somewhere nearby. *What's he doing?* she thought. *Announcing himself? Surely, he knows better than that!* She began to squirm on the leather of the seat, feeling a little exposed in the car with her underwear on show for the whole world to see. She looked out of the window at the pink panties currently flapping, rain-soaked, against the window, and made a decision. Mr Turnbull had had his chance, and he had now missed the golden opportunity that so many of the faculty had taken before him.

She grabbed at the small piece of the underwear that was caught inside the car and wound the window down with her other hand. As she did, a strong wind whipped up taking hold of the undergarment, and a ridiculous game of tug-of-war ensued as she struggled to hold the fabric.

A shadow passed between her and the dim light of the night.

This was something she hadn't been expecting, and it scared her. She let go of the underwear just as the wind died, and they fell, unceremoniously, to the ground. With panic rising in her stomach, she looked around her immediate vicinity but couldn't see anything out of the ordinary. *Must have been a branch in the wind,* she thought, harrumphing loudly. She opened the car door to find out where her panties had landed—she didn't want to leave any evidence of her being here. They were lying, totally out of place, in a muddy puddle. The bright pink of the garment contrasting with the dull brown of the mud they were submerged in. She leaned back into the car, wanting something to cover her head with, knowing she was going to have to retrieve them. There was no way they could be left there; they had her name written in the back of them for one thing, an old habit from her school days.

There was a newspaper languishing on the back seat. As she reached to grab it, a noise, that was most definitely *not* the rain falling on the trees around, her caught her attention. It sounded like someone creeping through the bushes around her.

It came again. Whoever it was, it was clear they were not creeping, or even trying to cover their tracks, it sounded like they were blundering their way through the undergrowth. To her, it sounded as if they were in a hurry. *Maybe the night isn't a blow-out after all,* she thought as she sat back in the seat, suddenly comfortable being half-naked again. With a salacious smile creeping across her face, she began to ease the seat back and hitch up her skirt.

~~~~

Mr Turnbull instantly regretted thumping the horn of the car. The last thing he wanted to do was attract attention to himself out here on Cemetery Road. He had absolutely no reason to be out here, and if he had to explain himself to Mrs Turnbull, he knew he'd crack under questioning. She was a skilled interrogator, and he'd never been a good liar. He decided that the only thing he could do was get out and assess the damage. Hopefully, he would be able to push the car out of the ditch, and then he could make up some story or other about why he was wet and muddy when she inevitably asked him about his state.

As he opened the door, a blast of rain caught him, and he was instantly soaked. 'No point *not* going out there now, is there?' he grumbled, pulling his jacket collar up to his ears.

It turned out he wasn't as wet as he thought he was, and the moment he stepped out of the car, the rain drenched him again. He slumped his shoulders, fixed his collar one more time, and waded around the car to inspect the extent of the damage. He let out a wet, bubbling sigh as he saw that the two front wheels were lodged firmly in the streaming ditch at the side of the road.

He leaned back on the car and cursed. 'Fucking weak-willed dick,' he spat. 'If I'd stayed at the dance, I wouldn't be in this mess.' He folded his arms and contemplated his predicament. 'It's all her fault,' he moaned, kicking the car behind him.

Something out in the field caught his eye.

It was a light.

'Oldman's house,' he marvelled. 'He'll have a tow truck, or at least his wife will. Neither of them will ask questions about why I'm out here.' Inside, he was rejoicing. He might be able to save the night, and maybe his marriage, after all. Even though he knew it was like locking the stable door after the horse had bolted, he fished out an umbrella from the trunk of the car. He locked the vehicle, opened the umbrella, and trudged his way towards the light at the end of the road.

~~~~

Ms Wellborn had been sat in the car with her skirt hitched up, displaying her lady bits for all to see, for a couple of minutes now. She had never been left waiting this long in her entire career as a loose woman, and that was some career.

With another harrumph, she pulled down her skirt and wiped the condensation from the window. *That should be passion steam,* she thought crossly as she continued to wipe. Once the window was clear, she saw a silhouette of someone standing in the bushes.

By the shape of the shadow, she guessed that it was a man.

She thought for a moment that maybe she should be frightened, out here, in the middle of nowhere, alone in a storm. But Ms Wellborn was a connoisseur of fine romance, and erotica, novels as well as being a raving nymphomaniac. She had been waiting for the 'mysterious stranger' scenario to come along all her life. Stuck in a stricken car in the middle of the woods, rescued by a muscular, hot mechanic who wanted to fix her car before fixing her.

She was up for that!

Winding her window down a little, she peered out into the night. The man was still there, standing in the pouring rain. He didn't look like he'd moved, not even a rippling muscle. *So, this is what your heart thrashing against your chest feels like,* she pondered, as tingles began to course from all areas of her body, all of them heading in the same direction.

Down.

They were rushing towards the place she wanted them to rush to, the place where she knew they would be most appreciated.

'Hey, mister,' she shouted from the window, fixing some of her hair behind her ear. 'Could you help a damsel in distress?'

Her voice caught the attention of the man, and for the first time since she'd noticed him, he moved his head.

'I think I might be having a little bit of engine trouble, and, being a poor, defenceless woman, out here all alone, I was wondering if you could take a quick look underneath my hood, so to speak.' She was using her best 'little girl lost' voice, which she had used on many a man in the past. *It never fails,* she thought with a saucy smile.

'I would be very grateful if you did. Very grateful indeed!'

As the man in the bushes turned his head and looked at her, Ms Wellborn took in a deep gasp!

~~~~

'Oldman? Is that you? Hello... Hello!' Mr Turnbull shouted as he staggered down the river that had once been a road. The person he was shouting to was skulking in the shadows of the bushes. It looked to him like they were trying to hide but not doing a very good job of it. 'I can see you there. I was wondering if you had a truck, or something to help me. My car's stuck in a ditch,' he shouted through the roar of the rain. Whoever it was either didn't hear him or was ignoring him. 'Hello! I asked if you had a truck. I need some help,' he shouted a little louder.

This got the man's attention, and he stepped out of the shadows. As he did, Mr Turnbull breathed a sigh of relief as he saw that it was Oldgirl, not Oldman. He was glad because he knew out of the two of them, Oldgirl would be the one who would be able to fix his car. If he had needed a recipe for soufflé or some of his clothes darned, then Oldman would have been the one he needed. But Oldgirl had the knowledge, and the brawn, to help him out of his current pickle. 'Oh, thank God it's you. My car's stuck in a ditch a little way back. Can you help me?'

It was then he noticed the purple lights that were reflecting in her eyes. At first, he thought nothing of them, but when she didn't answer, or even acknowledge that he had asked her a question, he began to feel a

76

little uneasy. Then he noticed all the other little purple lights dotted around, glowing, and flickering in the darkness.

A worm of panic began to wriggle in his stomach. He knew a little about nature, being a biology teacher by profession, and he couldn't think of anything natural that glowed the same sickly purple he was witnessing here. His gaze shifted back to Oldgirl, and the worm in his stomach twisted again. He saw her for the first time in the light of his own adjusted eyes.

What he saw terrified him.

Her face was ripped and torn. Flaps of skin hung from her cheeks, and her nose was gone, leaving a dark hole in the centre of her ravaged face. The way the flesh around the hole was ragged and raised, he guessed it had been bitten off. The top of her head was exposed, like the brain itself had been attacked. She shuffled in the darkness, taking a step towards him. That was when his fear broke. He turned away from the hideous sight, back towards the safety of his car. To his dismay, several more of the purple lights had gathered, impeding his retreat.

The worm in his stomach was dancing now.

Ghouls surrounded him. Ghouls that looked like they ought to be rotting in the ground, not stalking the fields of Kearney, scaring biology teachers who had been on their way for a small, innocent tryst.

'Who are you?' he asked, taking a step away from the purple-eyed monsters surrounding him. 'What do you want?'

He felt the reassuring trunk of an old sturdy tree behind him and attempted to press himself into it. He closed his eyes and wished he could become a part of the tree, to melt into the bark, climb inside and hide from whatever was happening around him.

He opened his eyes again, and instantly wished he'd kept them closed.

Mr Turnbull had known Oldgirl for quite a few years. Most of the town did. She and her husband were pillars of the community. He knew how ugly she was, *or had been, in life,* he added in his head, but the sight of the thing that she had become, bearing down on him with her mouth open and vile, but dangerous teeth gnashing and snapping at him, he knew would give him nightmares for the rest of his life.

However long that might be!

She said just one word. That one word was enough to make his knees buckle and make him slip down the tree into a crouching position with his hands over his head.

Oldgirl, and her motley looking crew, descended on him. The word that they kept repeating was…

'BRAINS!'

Only, the way they said it, it sounded more like 'BRRRRRAAAAAAIIINNNNNNSSSSSS!'

~~~~

Purple eyes.

They took her breath away at first. She had never, in all her years, seen anything so… beautiful. 'Oh my,' was all she managed to utter as she reached over to unlock the car's passenger door.

The shift of the suspension springs squeaked as she waved to catch the attention of the stranger. 'Hey, mister, you look like you'll catch your death out there. Why not hop in here where it's warm and dry?' she shouted after winding her window all the way down.

In the dim light of the night, all she could see was that he was naked from the waist up and had brilliant, glowing purple eyes. Both things were OK with her. In fact, they enhanced the sexy feelings in the pit of her stomach, and further south.

She opened the door and the light in the cabin turned on, instantly transforming the windows into almost perfect reflective mirrors. These mirrors blocked her view around the exterior of the vehicle, hiding the fact that her car was currently surrounded by more of the glowing purple eyes.

'Come on, mister,' she shouted. 'I don't bite… unless that's what you're into, of course,' she concluded, putting the sass into her voice that, in her experience, always got her what she wanted.

The man began to shuffle forward, and a satisfied grin spread across her face. She pushed the door open and eased back in her chair. As she did, the cabin lights flicked off again. In her lust for this scenario, and for the strange man with the fiery eyes, she never noticed the myriad of purple lights flickering around outside in this dark rainy night.

Her mystery man leaned in.

She looked deep into the glowing purple of his eyes, and her heart thrashed in her chest again. She didn't think she had ever seen anything so *sexy* in her entire life. *Why the Hell have I been messing about with that fumbling idiot Turnbull when all this time, this guy has been wandering around the woods?* she thought.

As he climbed into the car, she saw past the cuts and bruises that laced his skin. She ignored the injuries, and the bite marks, that gored his face and head. There was more to a man than loose flaps of rotting skin hanging from his face. Her lust was burning for his fiercely blazing eyes. The animal grunts and moans coming from his snapping, animated mouth were turning her on.

Throwing off what little morals she had, she flung herself at him. She didn't care about the stink issuing from him, or his cold wet skin, or the slimy, grabbing hands that were scratching at her. All she cared for was the passion throbbing inside her; the feel of her sexual butterflies flapping torrents of gossamer wings against her most intimate parts. Without even thinking, her hands were tugging at what was left of his trousers, loosening his belt and pulling at the sodden garments, itching to get at what was inside.

All she knew was that she needed this brute of a man inside her, and she needed him now.

Once his trousers were free, she felt the heat and the solidity of his member in her hands, and her head bent low. It didn't matter to her that he smelt like he'd been dead for years, she thought it was a sexy musk. All she could think about as her head drew the filthy, stinking penis closer to her mouth was that her 'mystery man' scenario was finally coming true.

'BRRRRRAAAAAAIIINNNNNNSSSSSS!' he growled.

'Oh yeah, baby,' she muttered, licking her lips. 'Brains all the fucking way!'

Realisation dawned on her then, it slapped her in the face, and she hesitated. The disgusting, dripping penis was less than an inch from her mouth. *What the Hell am I doing?* she thought as she looked at the filthy member in her hand. Her throbbing lust, her wandering in the craziness of her own fantasy, subsided, as she came to her senses.

Just a little too late.

The scream, issuing from deep within her chest, was cut short as her fantasy man opened his dangerous jaws wide, maybe too wide for his lips, which split and tore, coating his teeth with thick black goo, before biting into the back of her head.

A spray of fresh, red blood splashed across the windows.

Within seconds, the car was full as beings of various states of decay piled inside, all of them after just one thing.

Head!

15.

'WELL, THAT WASN'T as bad as I thought it was going to be,' Jason said over the hubbub in the changing room behind the stage. 'I thought we were going to be hammered due to the lack of cheerleaders.'

'Did you see everyone cheering?' Razor asked, his cheeks still flush from grinning.

'Especially the girls,' Hank replied, sitting down, and fanning himself with a shin pad he'd found in his bag. 'I'm glad Betty wasn't there now. She'd have my nuts if she'd seen all those chicks looking at me.'

Rob gave him a playful dig in the arm, but even a playful dig from Rob nearly knocked him off his feet. 'Watch your mouth, dude. That's my sister you're talking about!'

'I know, I know,' Razor replied rubbing his wound. 'I was only saying. It's not like I'm going to do anything about it, is it?'

'Just because you're chained to the fence, doesn't mean you can't bark at the cars, dude!' Kevin shouted, punching Hank in the other arm.

'Ow, fuck guys,' he shouted as the others laughed.

'Seriously, though, is no one worried about the girls? There's no way they'd have missed this tonight. Something must be wrong.' Jason had stripped down from his football uniform and was pulling on the tuxedo that his mother had rented for him, especially for tonight. White jacket, white waistcoat, white trousers, with a black shirt underneath. He'd made a fuss about her making him wear it, but deep down, secretly, he knew that Suzi would love him in it. *And out of it too,* he grinned.

'I know what you mean,' Brad said joining him by the lockers. He was putting on his tux too. 'Both Turnbull and Wellborn have gone looking for them, and neither have come back.'

'Do you really think those two are out there looking for them?' Kevin asked. 'We all know he'll be balls deep into her by now. My mom says she's a ho, and he's an idiot for going with her.'

'How do you know all this?' Jason asked, spitting on a black shoe, and buffing it with his football jersey.

'I heard mom and dad talking while they were making dinner the other night. They didn't know I was there.'

'That was probably just your dad trying to take the heat off himself for banging it into her at the last school disco,' Rob replied, laughing.

Kevin's cheeks flushed. He was laughing along, but his eyes told a different story. 'Yeah? Well, that was only because your mother was on the rag that week,' he retorted.

It was time for Rob's cheeks to flush.

Jason could see were this was heading, and he jumped in between the two larger boys. 'Guys, we've got bigger things to worry about than who's banged whose mom. Seriously, the girls wouldn't have missed tonight. It's all Suzi's been going on about for weeks. Something must have happened. We need to go and find them.'

'Have you seen the weather out there?' Razor asked, pointing towards the frosted over window. 'Your white jacket won't last five seconds in that, big guy.'

He looked where his friend was pointing, and his shoulders slumped.

'I've got to take this suit back on Monday. My dad had to pay twenty bucks deposit. He needs those twenty bucks back, or it'll come out of my allowance,' Hank said, looking out of the window with the others.

'You're right,' Jason conceded. 'Come on, the band will be taking a break in a minute. Let's get in there and mingle. The girls will be here before we know it.'

'Good idea, man,' Brad said slapping him on his back.

Within ten minutes, all six of them were suited and ready to disco with the rest of the school.

'We all good for this?' Jason shouted.

'Fuck, yeah,' was the overriding reply. It was their battle cry before a game.

'OK then, let the fun begin!'

~~~~

The six friends pushed open the doors to the main hall, and walked out together, followed closely behind by the rest of the team. They timed it perfectly to walk out just as the final song in the band's first set finished.

Everyone in the room began to clap, cheer, and whistle. For just a few moments, the boys forgot all about the missing cheerleaders.

16.

OUT IN THE tumultuous rain, on a river that used to be a road running parallel to a dark cemetery where past residents of the town of Kearney, Arkansas, used to be buried before recently awaking with a hunger for brains, there was an overturned car. The car was in danger of succumbing to the never-ending flash-flood that was battering it and the mud that came with it. Around the upturned vehicle, there was no other sign of life, or indeed any casualties of the accident that had caused the car to flip.

The night was dark, and the clouds were turbulent. The sky looked to be in a very bad mood indeed and was attempting to take it out on the ground below, mostly by drowning it.

The flood had washed away the broken glass from the accident, along with any other debris, pushing it all down river and away towards who-knew-where. All that remained was the car and the purple mud running downhill.

There was no sound of wildlife. No birds were singing in the trees, no animals scurrying away, attempting to save themselves, and their families, from the downpour. All was silent except for the rush of water and the sound of the incessant rain on the trees.

In the middle of the road, just opposite the overturned vehicle, a bubbling began from somewhere beneath the surface of the mud plain. At first, it was barely noticeable, and if there had been any observers, they certainly wouldn't have noticed that the bubbles were forming a circle. Or at least, they wouldn't have noticed until the bubbles became increasingly prevalent.

Then the shape could be observed.

It was indeed a circle.

The water that was mixed with the purple mud began to flow away from the bubbles as mounds of earth formed beneath the surface. Six molehills erupted from the makeshift river.

A hand broke free from one of them.

It grasped at the air. The skin on the hand looked like it used to be a luscious mocha but was now a pale imitation, much like the underbelly of a fish. The fingers flexed and stretched upwards towards the night, as if the owner of the hand was attempting to grasp the rain.

At the end of the fingers were perfectly manicured fingernails.

17.

THE CHEERING CROWD had calmed down after the football players made their entrance. The band were putting their instruments away and getting ready to tuck into the beers they had hidden in the back of their van. 'I put them in a gym bag with some ice, so they should be nice and cold right about now,' Keith said as he stowed his drumsticks in the small sleeve at the side of his kit.

'Man, for someone so dumb, you have some good ideas every now and then,' Geoff said, clapping him on the back.

'We need to put some background music on while we're out there. Do you have that disco tape?' Chris asked while searching through his pockets for the elusive packet of cigarettes he knew was in there somewhere.

'It's already in the player. It should kick in in a moment,' Bruce replied.

'Right on,' Geoff said with a smile. 'Now let's go and make a dent in those tins.'

'Don't make a dent in them,' Keith protested. 'When you open them, the beer will go everywhere.'

'Keith, if you had brains, you'd be dangerous,' Bruce said, walking down the stage steps.

On the dance floor, they were greeted by barrage of high school girls. They knew this would happen, it did at every school gig they did. Each of them would tell anyone who'd listen that the sole reason anyone gets into a band in the first place was for the chicks.

'Ladies… Ladies, you need to line up. We can't make all of you happy at the same time,' Bruce said with a grin spreading across his face.

'But,' Keith added. 'We will try our very best. But first, ladies, we need to smoke and to drink some alcohol. Who would like to join us?'

A few of the shyer girls began to back away. Once again, this was nothing new. A few of the hard-core stayed. The band members knew that these were the ones for the taking. 'All right, ladies,' Geoff said with a smile and a clap of his hands. 'Let's see where this party takes us.'

The remaining girls giggled and looked around for their chaperones, either Mr Turnbull or Ms Wellborn. Neither were about.

It was indeed party time!

'Are you going to get changed or something?' one of the girls asked, looking Bruce up and down.

Bruce smiled and shook his head. 'Oh no, sweet lady. The demon of funk is always in character,' he replied with a smirk.

'Oh,' the girl replied with a grimace. 'In that case, I'll be over here with the guy playing bass!'

Geoff beamed as he put his arm around the girl and led her towards the door. He spared just one small look back at Bruce, all alone with his shoulders slumped and looking down at his own ridiculous boots. He tipped him a wink before disappearing with the grinning girl.

~~~~

Three of the band members left the main hall with three young, but at least in Keith's mind, totally bad-ass girls. In the hall, the dancing had continued. Bruce's disco tape was going down a storm. Even better than the band had done. None of them were particularly bothered by this. They knew that disco was a fad, and once that Saturday Night Fever film had left the cinemas, then the disco fever that had spread across the nation would be over, and everyone could get back to listening to melodic rock. But, for now, the bass driven funk of disco was blaring through the hall. All the boys thought they were John Travolta, but without the dance moves, and all the girls were mooning over them as they writhed and strutted on the dancefloor.

'I can't go out there,' one of the young girls protested. 'It'll totally ruin my hair,' she said, running her hands through her perfectly coiffured locks.

'Same here,' another said. 'That rain will kill this dress,'

'I don't mind going, as long as you're with me,' a small girl with tightly cut black hair and a short, dress purred as she clung to Keith's arm.

Keith smiled and winked to the rest of the band. He raised his eyebrows and smiled. 'Looks like I'll be going to get the beer then. Why don't you lot take these girlies into the back room? I can't see us being *too* long,' he said with a smile aimed at the petite girl on his arm. 'Maybe about fifteen minutes, give or take.'

The others nodded and held out their arms to their girls. 'Ladies, shall we?' Geoff asked as a girl linked her arm in his. There was much giggling as Keith and his newest lady friend watched them go.

~~~~

'Come here, wrap this around you!' Keith said, taking off his denim jacket and draping it over his companion's shoulders. *You know what you're getting yourself into here?* he thought, but it wasn't what he said. 'It's only about fifty yards away.' He indicated towards the van sitting in the packed parking lot. 'I'll run and get it open. OK?'

'I'll be right behind you,' she replied with a wink.

I fucking love high school girls, he thought, stepping out into the rain. As he got to the van, he fished the keys out of his pocket and unlocked the door. He got in and unlocked the passenger door for his guest. Within moments, they were both sheltered from the rain in the front seats.

'So, about those beers,' he said, grinning.

'OK, these are the rules,' she said suddenly, taking him by surprise. 'I'm not going all the way with you. I'm saving that for someone who's not the drummer of a high school band. Second and third base are good to go, and if I feel like it, I'll give you head. We need to be back inside in at least fifteen minutes, or my little sister will get nervous. I'm her chaperone. Our mom wouldn't let her out on her own, in case she got involved with the band. So, if you're going to kiss me, I suggest you get on with it.'

Keith, never one to let an opportunity pass him by, jumped at his chance. They were necking heavily within a minute of getting into the van. Her dress was undone at the back within two minutes, and the zipper at the front of his jeans was undone within the third.

It was shaping up to be a good night for Keith.

~~~~

Outside in the rain, unbeknown to the lovers in the rocking van, purple, glowing eyes were hungrily watching their every move. There were a lot of them, hidden in the trees, or in the bushes, or in the shadows. They were attracted to the barn, and to the van; anywhere that was giving off the scent of brains.

Like a decaying, stinking wave, they advanced on the vehicle in the parking lot, the one with the steamed-up windows.

~~~~

'I don't even know your name,' Keith whispered, breathlessly, as the girl kissed his chest, taking extra time, and extra care, to bite and suck on his nipples. Every nip sent a surge of shivers up and down his torso.

'Do… you really… want to… know it?' she asked between bites. Her hands had ventured down further than his chest, a lot further, and with every bite came a small but firm squeeze. It was a very interesting combination.

His eyes rolled into the back of his head as he relaxed into the seat. 'I don't… OH JESUS!... believe that I doOOOOOH!' he shouted as her head bent lower, towards his crotch. His hand banged against the window a couple of times as her tongue began to do things that he'd never had done to him before.

~~~~

The van had caught the attention of most of the things outside. Their purple eyes were glowing fiercely as the scent of brains coming from the inside sent them into a frenzy. Their numbers had been sufficiently increased as more and more of them had been called to the crusade, and they had added quite a few more along the way. It was too much for them to resist.

'BRRRRRAAAAAAIIINNNNNNSSSSSS!'

The monster leading the horde of the undead hissed as it shuffled towards the shaking van. The others behind it agreed on their destination.

A wall of ghouls, all of them sporting radiant, purple eyes, advanced on the hapless teenage meals inside.

~~~~

'What was that?' Keith asked, sitting up on the seat for a moment.

'It's called a blow-job,' the girl with the dark hair said, wiping her mouth.

'No, not that,' he said, pushing her off him a little as he rubbed his arm on the condensation on the inside the window. 'I thought I heard something outside.'

'Probably one of your buddies trying to get in on the action. Or maybe just wanting to have a little perv.' She sat up and began to button-up her undone blouse.

'I don't think it was them, they usually just run up and bang on the windows, and shit.'

The girl looked at him and raised her eyebrows. 'Usually?'

Keith looked at her with a wide grin. 'Yeah, usually. This isn't my first rodeo, you know, and I've got a feeling that you've been around the block a few times too, baby.' He laughed at her shocked expression before turning his attention back outside the van and to the noise he'd heard. 'It sounded like someone was growling out there.'

The girl had lost all interest in what was happening and was fixing her panties underneath her skirt. 'For your information, dude,' the last word was spat, like an accusation. 'I don't go around giving blow-jobs to every... JESUS CHRIST!' The last two words were shouted.

Keith smiled and turned towards her. 'So, does that make me your first Jesus Christ?' he asked. The smile on his face was short lived as he saw her expression. His eyes followed the direction she was looking and saw what had scared her so much. 'Holy fuck,' he uttered as the purple glow from outside permeated through the condensation on the windows, bathing her in its glow. 'What the Hell is that?'

He looked out of his own window and saw the very same purple light. It was coming through the windshield too. 'What is that?' he whispered.

'I don't know, but I'm not waiting around to find out,' the girl said, fumbling for the latch on the door. The instant it opened, a foul stink of decay filled the cabin, and Keith and the girl both retched.

'What the fuck is that funk?' he asked, not really wanting to know.

He was answered with a roar, followed by a scream.

He turned his head to see what was happening, just in time to witness the girl being dragged out of the van, into the rain-soaked parking lot, by something that he could only describe as... 'a dead looking fuck!'

'Keith, help... help me,' she screamed as the thing scratched and grabbed at her. The drummer watched helplessly as his date was dragged out of the van, where the thing dragging her was joined by a number of other, similar looking nightmares. He knew he should do something; he should jump out and start to beat the things away from her with his fists and his feet and any other weapon that he could find.

But he didn't.

All he could do was sit and watch as the things tore off the girl's clothes and began to bite her, paying extra attention to her head.

'BRRRRRAAAAAAIIINNNNNNSSSSSS!'

He thought he heard them shouting *brains* to each other, but that seemed like a crazy thing to think. *Anymore crazy than sitting here watching the chick who was blowing me only moments ago getting eaten alive by dead looking fucks?* he asked himself.

He knew the answer.

He scrabbled at the latch on his own door. He knew that once they'd finished with her—*Shit, I don't even know her name*— they were going to start coming for him. He needed to get out of the van and back to the safety of the barn.

He caught the latch and opened the door. As he did, a couple of the beasts that had been languishing outside were pushed away with the force. He glanced around and was dismayed to find a herd of the *shiny-*

92

eyed-dead-looking-fucks between him and the door to the hall. 'Fuck,' he muttered under his breath, as the decision to go was thrust upon him by one of the things reaching out with a bony, blood-, meat-, and gore-covered fingers. The ugly thing snapped its jaws, and Keith was disgusted to see a chewed-up eyeball fall from its mouth.

The thought of the girl, who was now lying on the swampy ground being eaten by God only knew what, having his penis in her mouth merely minutes ago churned his stomach, but he knew he had to put all such thoughts behind him, at least for now. He needed to get away from the van and into the barn. *Safety in numbers,* he thought.

With that in mind, he made a run for it.

He was out of the van in a flash, running through the flooded parking lot. The barn was less than fifty yards away, and he thought he was going to make it.

'Oh shit,' he panted. 'I forgot the beer.'

He paused for a few seconds, in two minds whether to go back and get it, but then decided that when he got back inside, and told everyone what had just happened, beer would be very low on everyone's priorities.

As he started running again, he swerved out of the way of one of the *dead-looking-fucks* coming right at him. This thing had its arms held out towards him, grasping for him, swiping at him. What caused him to lose his balance and splash into the muddy waters of the parking lot wasn't the fact that the thing looked like it had been dead for fifty years, but the fact that it had a pair of women's bright pink panties over its head. The sight had been so absurd that he almost forgot where he was running to and what he was running from. The next thing he knew, he was sprawled on the ground with some *dead-looking-fucks* gaining on him.

'BRRRRRAAAAAAIIINNNNNNSSSSSS!'

He knew he didn't have time to get up. They would be on him before he even got to his knees. There were three of them leading the

93

shuffling pack. Even though they were moving slowly, they were deceptively agile. Nevertheless, he knew he had to try. He didn't want to end up like ... *fuck, I really wish I'd gotten her name.*

As he made it onto his knees, he felt the first of the cold, wet hands grab him. Not only were they agile, they were also very strong. He was pulled up towards the face of the gnashing, purple-glowing-eyed beast.

'BRRRRRAAAAAAIIINNNNNNSSSSSS!' it hissed as its other hand reached for his head.

'BRRRRRAAAAAAIIINNNNNNSSSSSS!' a second beast croaked as it grabbed him by the shoulder, spinning him around.

Pain piqued as the bite from a third monster pierced the skin on his neck and blood began to ooze from the wound. His legs went weak, and he felt like he was about to fall again. There were more hands on him now, but he had only felt one bite. He dared to open one of his eyes and was confused to see that the three things holding him seemed to be conducting an in-depth conversation regarding him.

'BRRRRRAAAAAAIIINNNNNNSSSSSS?' one of them growled. To Keith, it sounded like a question.

'BRRRRRAAAAAAIIINNNNNNSSSSSS!' the second one replied. Blood seeping from its mouth as it spoke.

Keith wasn't shocked to see it was his blood.

'BRRRRRAAAAAAIIINNNNNNSSSSSS!' the third replied with a comical shrug. It was like it was confirming the question that the first one had asked.

Then, without any further ado, he felt himself being pushed roughly to the ground.

Back in the mud, he looked up to see the three monsters shuffling away from him, one of them now chewing on the pink panties it had pulled down from its head. Keith didn't need an invitation to get up and away from where he was lying. Whatever gift, or reprieve, he had just been granted was not going to be lost on him. In a flash, he was back on his feet and zooming towards the double door that he had exited less than twenty minutes ago—but which felt like a lifetime ago. He checked the bite on his shoulder and was relieved to see that it was only a flesh wound. The bastard thing had managed to break the skin, but it didn't seem all that bad.

I'll survive! he thought as he crashed through the big doors.

18.

THE THICK CLOUDS shifted and grinded in the sky. Even though a tremendous amount of rain had fallen on the small town, there was no indication they would be dissipating anytime soon.

Except for a very brief respite.

For just a few moments, there was the smallest of gaps. Through that gap, a single shaft of almost perfect moonlight managed to cut through the gloom. As the night was so dark, the thin sluice resembled a ray of sunlight as its beam pierced the darkness, brightening the scene below.

Six large hills of disrupted earth had appeared in the road next to the overturned car. From these six hills had emerged six beings, all of them currently standing, motionless, in the rain, looking upwards, towards the break in the clouds.

From behind, they looked normal. Just six girls, wearing cheerleader uniforms, standing in the rain, looking up to the clouds, receiving instruction.

The girl at the front stood out from the others due to her large afro hairstyle. But this wasn't the only reason she was different. There was an air of leadership about her as she stood, as if defying the rain, with her head held high. Her four eyes gleamed with the same silver radiance as the moon beam that was shining down on her.

The two girls directly behind her, their heads also looking upwards, also had two sets of eyes, and these were glowing too. The first had long, dangerous looking braids in her hair. They were swinging in the breeze of the storm. With each swipe came a dangerous swoop and snap. The second girl looked to be normal from her waist upwards, but from the waist down, she was very different. Her legs were thick, toned, and muscular, very muscular, almost too muscular. They looked like they had been carved from marble.

Behind them were another three girls, again all looking up to the sky with their double sets of glowing eyes. The first of these appeared to have horns protruding from her head; horns that were joined together by a thick metal chain. The second was as big, and as muscular, as a Russian hammer-thrower. Her fingers twitched eagerly, as if in anticipation of necks to crack. The final girl would have looked like a regular cheerleader if it hadn't been for the impressive wingspan of the long, white, angel-like wings on her back.

The shaft of moonbeam illuminated them, bathing them in its silvery glory, elongating their shadows on the dark, muddy ground.

Eventually, the moment passed, and the clouds began to rumble and tumble back over themselves. The beam faulted for just a moment, as if it was reluctant to leave, before flittering away, and the darkness once again prevailed.

The rain continued to fall, but it didn't bother these six mysterious figures. In fact, it didn't seem to even touch them. For six people who had inexplicably risen from the ground, their short skirts, sneakers, and cheerleader sweaters didn't appear very dirty. As a matter of fact, they looked almost new.

The girl at the front with the extraordinary large hair raised her hand as if signalling the rest of the girls behind her.

They all followed suit.

'Give me an L,' she shouted, her voice sounding like the combination of many voices condensing into one.

The five girls behind her obeyed her command. A loud 'L' rose from them in perfect unison.

'Give me an I,' she continued.

The girls shouted their 'I' into the night.

'Give me an O,' she continued.

Once again, they obeyed her order.

'Give me and N.'

'N,' they replied.

'Give me an S,' her strange voice never once wavered.

The 'S' in response was as loud and as strong as the very first 'L'.

'What do we have?' she shouted, her voice the voice of hundreds, if not thousands, in one.

'LIONS!' was the unified response. It was shouted so loud that the windows of the overturned car, the ones were *not* already smashed in the accident, all shattered at once. Gravestones that had stood in the cemetery for hundreds of years began to shake in their footings, before falling as if knocked over by a powerful blast.

As one, the girls began to walk, keeping their triangular formation perfectly. It was as if they had practiced this walk for years.

As they strutted, they headed towards a large, well-lit barn off in the distance. Six sets of double eyes stared, unblinking, at the light. The girl with the large hair clicked her fingers, and the others followed suit. They continued to walk in formation towards their destination. Their pale skin glowing in the dim, purple glow of the storm.

Mutant Cheerleaders!

19.

KEITH CRASHED THROUGH the double doors. At first, no-one noticed him, even with his soaking wet, torn clothes seeped in blood. Everyone was far too busy dancing and enjoying themselves.

'Help me!' he shouted as he crawled along the floor.

Unfortunately for him—and as it turned out, for the revellers in the disco too—his shouts for help coincided exactly with the lyrics to the song playing over the speakers.

'Help Me!' the whole crowd shouted as Keith crawled, unnoticed, into the dance hall.

'Help me!' he shouted again, at precisely the same time the assembled students on the dance floor shouted the exact same thing.

He looked behind him, out the doors he had fallen through, towards the rain-soaked parking lot outside. There, he could see the blazing eyes of the undead, decaying cannibal bastards, milling around trying to follow him into the barn.

'We need to get these doors closed,' he screamed, just as the funked-up bass dropped on the song and everyone cheered. A circle broke out on the floor, and everyone began to strut their stuff in the centre.

'We're all going to die,' he shouted again, unheard by the revelling masses. He rolled his eyes and scrambled to his feet, launching himself at the doors. He managed to crash them closed just in time, as one of the rotting things had made it to the door and would have been inside if he hadn't slammed it in its face. As they closed, the thing managed to trap one of its arms between the two heavy wooden slabs. The force of the slam snapped the limb off, almost at the shoulder.

As the doors banged closed, the song playing over the speakers finished, and the only sound that could be heard was Keith shouting. 'And stay out, you dead looking fucks!'

Everyone turned to see the soaking wet drummer, bloody, and dishevelled, holding what looked like the severed arm of something that he had dug up from a graveyard, an old one.

As a blob of thick, black goo dripped from the exposed bone on the limb he was holding, a girl, who had only moments before been enjoying the disco beats of the number one song, 'Save Me (Dance Floor)', began to scream.

A few of the older students, Keith thought they might have been members of the football team, began to rush him. He fell back against the door and dropped the arm as if it had been a weapon and he was laying down his arms, so to speak. His eyes were wide and scared. 'Hold on,' he shouted. 'Hold the fuck on. I can explain everything.'

At that moment, there was a powerful bang on the doors. Its force propelled Keith from his defensive position, and into the path of the approaching mob. 'Listen to me. There're *things* out there. Things, I'm telling you!'

Another bang caused the large students to shift their focus from the wet and bloody drummer to the rattling door.

'We need to bar this with something. If they get in here, I'm telling you, they'll eat us, just like they did with…'

'With who?' one of the larger boys asked, staring at him.

'Oh Christ... I don't know what her name was,' he scolded himself. 'Like, whatshername... the girl I left with to get the beers.'

'You've got beers?' one of the other football players asked.

Keith wobbled his head. 'Well, erm... yes and no,' he answered.

'Well, you either have beer or you don't, man. There really is no middle ground.'

The door banged again, and everyone forgot about beer, for now.

'We need to get this barred,' Keith shouted, turning back to brace the door with his body. He looked around for something to hold it with. Nothing obvious jumped out at him, except for the torn arm lying on the floor before him. He bent down and picked up the rotting stump. He held it towards the others in the room, who were now watching his every move. All of them, without exception, recoiled at the sight of the filthy thing waving at them. He shrugged, then slotted the rotting appendage in between the two handles, creating a makeshift lock.

Another bang rocked the doors, and the arm bent at the elbow.

'What the Hell's out there?' the football player at the front of the pack asked. He was darker skinned than the others, and it looked like he was the leader.

'If I told you, you wouldn't believe me,' Keith panted as the door bang again.

'Try me,' he replied.

'I was out there, in the van. I was with that girl. One of your girls.'

'Ours?' the leader asked. 'What's her name?'

Keith rolled his eyes and wiped some of the water from his brow, leaving a swathe of red across his face. 'Man, don't fucking ask me that question,' he cried.

'So, where is she now?' another football type asked from behind the lead boy. This boy was almost as big as a tree.

Keith inhaled deeply. Another disco song had started up over the speakers, but no-one was dancing anymore. Everyone was gathered around watching what was happening. The song was 'Night Fever,' a song Keith particularly hated. He was glad when someone turned it off halfway through.

'Well,' he continued. 'We were getting our groove on. She was up for it, totally. The chick really did seem to dig drummers. I think she'd been around the block a few times, like, you know, she had all these rules and stuff—'

'Keith!' Bruce snapped. He was at the back of the football players, looking out of place in his cloak and sparkling outfit. 'Just tell us what the fuck happened, man,' he warned.

Keith nodded and caught his breath again. 'Well, we were getting it on when I heard a strange noise from outside. I thought it was one of you guys playing tricks on us. They do that sort of shit, even in rain like this. I told her not to, but she opened the door and was dragged out, by these... these...'

'These what?' one of the football players asked.

Keith looked up at the big one and swallowed, hard. 'Things,' was all he could think of as an accurate description.

'Things? Things? You're telling us that *things* took the girl you were making out with? Snatched her right out of your van?' the big one asked again. He was shaking his head.

Keith could see that his explanation was not going down well with the locals. 'They were dead looking fucks. They did this to me. Look,' he said pulling down his soggy t-shirt to show the bite-mark on his neck that was still leaking blood.

'Whoa!' the leader of the group gasped as he looked at the wound and stepped back a little.

'Man, that's one nasty hicky!' Bruce said, sucking in a deep breath. 'I'm glad I never went with that chick.'

102

'One of these *things* did that to you?'

'Yeah, exactly. One of the dead looking fucks.'

'What did they do to the girl?'

Keith's shoulders sagged. 'That's what I've been trying to tell you, man. They dragged her out of the van. They ate her.'

'Ate her?' Another football player asked, stepping forward.

'Yeah, ate her. They tried to eat me too. They kept going on and on about brains and shit. I don't know.'

'So why didn't they finish you? If they ate this girl you're telling us about, how did you survive?' the lead boy asked again.

'That'll be because he's fucking brainless,' Geoff said as he pushed through the gathered crowd. Everyone turned to look at him. 'Jesus Christ, Keith, what happened to you? That girl wasn't on her period, was she?' he asked, indicating towards the blood down his shirt.

'That's not funny, man,' he replied, with a humourless smile. 'I was very nearly eaten out there.'

'Eaten? Was she that good?' Geoff asked, looking around for the laugh that was not forthcoming. 'What is that on the door?' he asked. 'Is that an arm?'

'Yeah, it is. And right now, it's the only thing stopping the things out there from getting in here and doing the same to everyone else.' Keith replied. As he spoke, his face contorted into a wince, and he put his hand up to the bite on his neck, attempting to stem the ache, and throb, he could feel getting worse.

'Things? What things?' Geoff asked as he reached towards the arm in-between the door handles. Another heavy bang made him swerve his hand away.

'I'm fucking telling you. Don't move that... URGGGGH!' Keith didn't finish his sentence. What he did do was bend over, almost double, as hot, raging agony tore through his body. It stemmed from his neck before travelling both ways, up towards his head and down into his chest and stomach.

'Keith! Keith, man, what's up?' Geoff asked as Chris came running through the crowd to see what all the fuss was about. Bruce was behind him, wobbling in the stupid platform shoes he was still wearing.

'What the fuck?' Bruce sputtered as he saw his friend writhing in agony on the floor.

'I don't know. He's babbling on about some *things* out there biting him and eating the girl he was with,' Geoff explained.

'Wasn't he supposed to be doing the eating?' Bruce asked, playfully slapping Chris to get him to acknowledge the joke.

The leader of the football team ran over to the window. He put his head to the pane of glass and squinted as he covered his eyes, blocking out the glare of the lights from inside. 'There's something out there. It looks like some dudes joking around, though. Like they've all got little purple torches. All I can see is purple lights glowing in the dark.'

'Bastards,' Geoff said as he looked through the window too.

'Jason,' the big football student shouted towards the lead boy. 'Should we go out and put the fear of God up them?' he asked, slamming his fist into his hand with a grin stretching the whole width of his face.

'I don't know, Rob, there looks like quite a few of them. It might be best to wait this one out,' he replied, still looking out the window.

Another bang on the door alerted everyone to the fact that there *was* someone outside, and *that* someone was intent on getting inside.

'Can you see who that is?' a smaller boy asked.

'I can't see anyone, Razor. Just a load of purple lights bobbing around.' Jason turned away from the window and looked towards Rob and Razor. 'Why don't us three go and have a word with them. See what's up, and if they don't want to split, well, then we can just go ahead and—'

'Call the police,' an older voice piped up from the back of the room. It was Mr Smart, the assistant principal. In the absence of Mr Turnbull and Ms Wellborn, the old drunkard was the only responsible adult left at the party. It seemed that everyone had forgotten about him as they turned to see who was speaking.

'But, Mr Smart,' Jason began.

'I don't want to hear another word about it, Mr Fisher. We'll call the police, they'll come and clear up this criminal element, and that'll be the end of that. In my day, we never had shenanigans like this, with cavorting, and hooligans. We had nice, decent, Christian proms, where the boys asked the girls to dance, properly. None of this *disco* rubbish!' He pronounced the word disco as if it was a particularly nasty tasting piece of candy.

~~~~

Rob and Razor ignored the ramblings of the old man and looked to Jason for instruction. He gave them a small nod, Rob tipped him a wink in reply, and they both continued towards the door.

'Move that arm, Razor,' Rob ordered as they stood looking at the ugly thing.

'I'm not touching that. Who knows what diseases are all over it?' Razor was leaning in, inspecting the thing in the door handles. He could have sworn he'd seen it twitch. 'What if it's still alive?'

'Are you stupid?' Rob asked as he pushed his smaller friend aside. He reached out, meaning to grab it and fling it away from the door, but as he did, it *did* twitch. He jumped back. 'Jesus, fuck,' he shouted.

'See, I told you it was alive,' Razor cried, stepping back himself.

'But, if that's alive in here, then the things out there that the dude from the band was talking about…'

The cogs in Rob's slow brain were turning. If he hadn't been so scared, Razor would have thought it was funny and told all the other guys about it. But as it was, he was too busy trying not to think about the twitching stump holding the door closed to care about what the other guys would say.

Another bang from outside caused them both to jump.

'Oh fuck. Come on,' Rob said, not entirely convincingly. 'There's no way there are crazy monsters out there eating people. That shit only happens in crappy books written by dweebs. Come on, let's get out there and see where the girl, that drummer-boy was talking about, is,' Rob said, hoping his rousing speech would inspire Razor to offer to remove the arm.

It didn't.

'Oh, fuck this,' he shouted and grabbed the twitching arm, pulling it out of the handles. With the cold thing still in his grip, he looked over towards the others. They were all either too busy looking out the window or talking among themselves to notice what happened between him and Razor. He took special notice of the boys from the band, who were tending to their friend with the bite. He looked to be in some considerable pain as they pulled him to the side of the room. He gritted his teeth and exhaled. 'Come on. Let's get these doors open and see what's happening out there,' he muttered, attempting to convince himself more than Razor.

The arm was cold and clammy in his grip, and he wanted nothing more than to get the thing as far away from him as he could. 'If this is a joke, I'm going to rip that drummer a new one,' he spat, dropping the vile appendage onto the floor.

'I don't think it is, Rob. Look,' Razor pointed over to where the guy was now propped up against the wall. 'I don't think he's faking that, do you?'

Rob watched as the stricken drummer vomited over his band mates. There were plenty of 'Fuck's sakes' and 'Jesus Christs' being shouted, and more than a few of the girls ran away holding their mouths to stop their own vomit from spewing forth.

Razor stepped up and opened the double doors. 'Close this after we're gone, OK?' he shouted, trying to sound braver than he felt.

Jason nodded and made his way to the door. 'Be careful out there, man. I don't want to have to train up two new football stars, you dig?' he said with a smile.

Rob smiled back at him. 'Don't worry about us...'

'We'll be right back!' Razor finished.

~~~~

Outside, the rain was cold. The booming of the doors closing behind them made Razor turn and watch as they wobbled.

'I wish I'd brought my coat,' Rob said, running his fingers through his buzz-cut hair.

'Look at all this shit,' Razor said as he bent down to look at debris that was all over the steps leading up to the door. 'What is that?'

Rob hunkered down to look at it. 'I don't know, but if I was to hazard a guess, I'd say it looks like blood.'

'Isn't blood supposed to be red?' Razor asked, putting his finger in the brownish goo plastered over the steps. He sniffed the ooze before flicking it off his finger and pulling a face. 'That is gross,' he shouted, trying his best to keep the gag in his stomach from coming to fruition.

Rob hit him across the head. 'Don't be sticking your fingers into shit, fool,' he chastised.

'Why not? Your momma seems to like it,' Razor replied as quick as anything.

'Come on, you idiot. Let's see what we can see.'

Razor stood up and wiped his hand on the back of his trousers, grimacing at the vile substance that was sticking to his fingers. 'Are you sure your mom's not out here? Coz that smell really reminds me of—'

'Razor, you finish that sentence, I'll fucking eat you myself,' Rob warned.

Razor took the hint and backed off. He turned towards the barn and saw several people looking out the windows, all of them vying to get a look at what was happening. 'I'd rather be in there,' he said, looking up at the sky. 'At least it's dry and warm.'

'There's the van,' Rob said pointing to the large vehicle with its doors wide open. 'Let's take a look.'

Razor rolled his eyes and followed the bigger youth further from the safety of the barn.

~~~~

'I can't see the purple lights anymore,' Jason confirmed as he searched the parking lot, out of the window. 'But it looks like the guys have made it to the van.'

A noise from the other side of the room caught his attention. It was a scream, coupled with the disgusting, gurgling noise that was usually the precursor of a rather violent bowel movement.

'No fucking way,' came a shout as one of the band members stepped away from the drummer, who was still stooped against the wall. Jason thought it was the singer. 'Fuck, man. Why didn't you give me any warning, dude?' he shouted at the sick looking youth.

Is his name Keith? Jason thought as he watched him wipe something from his shirt and trousers, reluctantly. It looked like pink vomit, or it could have been blood. He couldn't tell from this far away. But the smell that was permeating around the room told him there was a good chance that it was neither blood, nor vomit, but something from a different orifice, one that was 'south of the mouth'.

'Has that boy messed himself?' Mr Smart shouted towards the rest of the band, who were fussing around their friend.

The singer, Geoff, looked over at him. 'What?'

'I asked if he's messed himself. If he has, you're going to have to remove him from the hall. It's stinking to high heaven and causing a public hygiene issue. We've got young ladies in here, for Heaven's sake.'

Jason turned away from the action inside the hall and looked back out the window. There was no longer any sign of his two friends in the gloomy parking lot, but he could make out that the doors to the van appeared to be closed. He scanned the lot for them again. His heart felt too heavy for his chest when he saw that the odd purple lights were making a reappearance, it had decided to take up residency in his stomach, instead. 'They're back,' he muttered, more to himself than to anyone else.

'Who are?' Mr Smart asked. 'The two boys I forbade to go out there in the first place? Just wait until I give them a good talking to.'

Jason looked around at the old man. His face was serious. His mouth merely a white scar across his old face. 'No, the kids, the ones with the purple lights,' he replied, doing his best to keep his anger at bay.

'They're not kids,' came a croaky voice from further down the hall. Jason was amazed that the whispery voice could travel across the strangely quiet hall. 'I keep telling you.'

It was the drummer.

Jason walked over towards him. The closer he got, the worse the stink was. *How are those guys managing to stand next to him?* he wondered as he watched Geoff wipe at the wet stain on his trousers. To Jason, Keith looked like he was dying. There was little, to no, colour in his face, except for the dark rings around his eyes. He also looked like he'd lost a lot of weight just in the few minutes since he'd come rushing back into the party. *Bringing all this shit with him,* he thought. 'So, if they're not kids playing around out there, then what are they?' he asked, getting as close to the dilapidated drummer as he could stand.

'They're the dead, and they've come back for us,' the young man replied. 'For vengeance!'

Jason noted, with more than a little unease, that there was a purple hint to the whites of the drummer's eyes. 'Vengeance for what?' he asked.

'For being alive,' Keith croaked, before beginning to cough. As the fit started, everyone who had managed to get close to him despite the stench stepped back. Blood spattered from his mouth with every cough. Geoff, the singer, caught a whole mouthful's worth all over his already stained shirt.

20.

THE BRIGHTNESS WAS closer now. The pounding beat that had been pulsing from the building had ceased. This did not deter the six strange girls who were walking in formation, clicking their fingers in complete rhythm with their steps.

Other noises had taken over the throbbing beat. These were screams and shouts for help. The girls' senses were not heightened to these but by the other noises, the ones that were hiding beneath the shouting and yelling, below the white noise of the rain. It was hardly more than a hiss, but it was one with a purpose. It was telling the world what they wanted to feed on...

'BRRRRRAAAAAAIIINNNNNNSSSSSS!'

The girls, now significantly changed from the ambitious, glamourous, boisterous teenagers they'd been an hour earlier, continued their strut.

Each had transformed, mutated, into something different. Something... better!

They were now Mutant Superhero Cheerleaders!

21.

'BRRRRRAAAAAAIIINNNNNNSSSSSS!'

'Will you quit that?' Rob snarled at Razor, who was leaning into the van the musicians had showed up in.

'Quit what?' Razor asked, looking up towards the bigger man, leaning into the passenger side, opposite him.

'BRRRRRAAAAAAIIINNNNNNSSSSSS!'

'That. Stop goofing around. We've got a job to do here. We need to find this girl.'

'Rob, the joke's not funny. You've been hissing the word *brains* for the last few minutes. I'm trying to concentrate here.'

'That wasn't me, it was you,' Rob snarled again, sounding more alarmed than Razor felt comfortable with. He knew now that his friend wasn't joking.

'Well, if it wasn't you...'

'BRRRRRAAAAAAIIINNNNNNSSSSSS!'

Both boys looked at each other, neither wanting to admit what they'd heard. Finally, Razor broke the silence. 'So, if it wasn't you, and I know it wasn't me...'

'Holy shit,' Rob shouted.

Razor looked up again, just in time to see Rob looking over his shoulder, his skin was the colour of three-day-old snow. His stomach dropped, and the hackles on the back of his neck stood up. *It's behind me, isn't it?* he thought, even though he had no idea what *it* could be.

'BRRRRRAAAAAAIIINNNNNNSSSSSS!'

That hiss came from behind him. He began to back away, pushing himself out of the van through the passenger side door.

'Rob,' Razor whispered.

He didn't answer; he just continued to stare past him.

'Rob,' he whispered again, irritation in his hushed voice.

Rob slithered out of the van, closing the door behind him.

'Where the fuck are you going, Rob?' Razor shouted.

Something grabbed him from behind.

Whatever it was, it was strong. Rough fingers gripped him by the back of his wet trousers and pulled him out of the van. He tried to grab hold of something, anything, to help him stay in the cabin. He gripped the steering wheel, but as he did, it spun, and he slipped even further.

'BRRRRRAAAAAAIIINNNNNNSSSSSS!'

Something tore into the back of his leg. The pain was tremendous, and he screamed. It took a moment or two for what had just happened to sink in. *I've been bitten,* he thought. *Who the fuck bites people in this day and age?* He screamed as hot surges of agony shot through his leg and up into his crotch. But it didn't stop there; it split into about sixty different tendrils of torture that had decided to take road trips through his entire body. The bite was then accompanied by another rough hand grabbing at him and, unbelievably, another bite. As the searing pain exploded through him again, he let go of the steering wheel and was pulled, effortlessly, and helplessly, out of the van. There was another explosion as his head hit the door mantle, before feeling the cold of the muddy ground caress his temple.

For a moment, a blissfulness sank through him as the pain in his body began to dull. Suddenly he wasn't in a cold, muddy parking lot being eaten alive by some unknown entity; he was on a football field in the warm sun. Several semi-naked cheerleaders were jumping up and down, shouting his name, as he ploughed his way down the final nine yards, speeding towards the goal line. As he crossed it, the scantily clad girls ran at him, mobbing him. He felt the delights of their silky, naked breasts rubbing up and down his face as they hugged and kissed him. Then the rest of his teammates ran over, they began to drag him away from the pleasures, and the nakedness, and thrust him high above their heads, chanting his name.

As quickly as it had appeared, the dream dissolved, as he was hauled cruelly from his euphoric vision, back into the reality of being devoured by creatures straight out of a cheap-ass movie.

'BRRRRRAAAAAAIIINNNNNNSSSSSS!'

The thing that was leaning over him had once been human. Maybe not even that long ago. His—or her, he couldn't tell—features were ugly, wrinkled, decrepit. There were deep cuts and nasty lacerations all over its face. Its eyes were glowing a perfect purple blaze. Blood poured from its mouth, and he could see a small dangle of something caught within the dangerous teeth that were gnashing at him. It took him a moment to focus on the small flap. Then, realisation dawned on him like a skillet whacking him in the face. He saw that it was a piece of his trousers, and attached to the material was a small piece of… him!

Keith was right, he thought. *There really are things out here.* 'Get off me, you freaky fuck,' he screamed, kicking out, trying to get whatever was on him, off. But the thing was far too strong and far too resilient to give up its meal that easy. As he kicked, it grabbed his foot and bit right through the leather of his shoe.

More pain surged as one, or even more, of his toes were bitten off.

Another fucked-up thing joined the buffet. This one looked like the first, and recognition dawned on him. It was Oldman, and Oldgirl.

Only they were different, still ugly, but a different kind of ugly.

'BRRRRRAAAAAAIIINNNNNNSSSSSS!' Oldman hissed.

'Whoa,' Razor shouted through the agony. 'Oldman! It's me, Razor. I used to help your wife in the fields. Razor! You know me, I play for the football team.' The thing that had once been Oldman looked at him. The purple fire in its eyes flickered. This moment gave Razor a moment of reprieve from the horror that was occurring. Maybe Oldman had recognised him after all. He sighed deep. That was when all the recognition, all the humanity, in Oldman's eyes dissipated, and they began to blaze the weird purple fire once more.

The thing Oldman had become roared as it opened its ugly mouth wide. 'BRRRRRAAAAAAIIINNNNNNSSSSSS!' it screamed, before bringing its dangerous teeth down onto Razor's face.

As the door to the van closed above him, Razor was transported, once again, to that sunny football field he'd been on earlier. The semi-naked cheerleaders were still there. He'd been dropped by the other team members, who were now all leaning over him. The topless cheerleaders were pushing their way through the crowd. With killer smiles on their gorgeous faces, they began to fawn over him, pawing him, licking him.

It was an enjoyable, blissful experience, until they started biting. His blood was pouring from their beautiful mouths, dripping between their perfect teeth, flowing, and pouring over their naked, perky breasts.

They bit until he felt nothing, ever again.

22.

'I CAN'T SEE either of them. But I can see those purple lights out there,' Hank shouted as he took up Jason's position at the window.

'Keep looking, they have to be out there somewhere,' Jason shouted back. He hadn't taken his eyes off Keith as more and more blood poured from his mouth. 'I think there's something seriously wrong with that guy.'

'Are you a doctor now?' Chris, from the band, asked as he distanced himself from the poorly drummer, obviously trying to stay out of the way of any further splurges, from either end of his friend's body.

Jason gave him a hard stare. 'No, I'm not, but look at him.'

Chris did as he was told and shook his head. 'Do you think we should call the police? Or an ambulance, or something?' he asked, all traces of sarcasm and fight had slipped from his voice.

'Let me take a look at the boy,' the older, slightly British voice of Mr Smart came from behind. Jason turned to see the small man striding towards him.

'I wouldn't get too—'

'Oh, Holy mother of Jesus,' the older man cursed as he stepped into the zone of stench coming from the injured boy. 'Let me see him,' he finished, pegging his nose with his fingers.

'I wouldn't get too close if I were you,' Jason continued as the teacher hunkered down to look at him.

'Hmm, what appears to the be the issue, boy?' the old man asked, the hand over his face muffling his words somewhat. He reached his other hand out towards him, to feel his brow as most people do when they see someone who looks ill. That was when Keith lifted his head. His eyes were suddenly a deep, blazing purple, and his mouth was open, wide. There was no colour in his skin, but he was strangely animated.

'BRRRRRAAAAAAIIINNNNNNSSSSSS!' he hissed in a croaked voice.

Mr Smart fell back, putting his hand behind him to stop himself from sprawling.

Keith took that moment to attack.

Like a coiled spring, the former drummer sprang forth and was on top of the old man before anyone knew what was happening. His wide-open mouth snapped closed, firmly over the old man's face. The shouts of pain and surprise were muffled by the thing that used to be Keith, looming over him, with his mouth tearing away at his face.

Everyone in the room stared dumbfounded as the younger man appeared to eat the older man.

From somewhere in the room, a single scream rang out. It was a female voice, and it set off two courses of events. Most of the other women in the hall began to scream in solidarity with the original, and it kicked the boys into action. Chris and Jason lunged forward and pushed Keith away from the cowering Mr Smart.

'What the fuck are you doing, man?' Chris shouted as he reached in, trying to lift his friend by the arms.

Keith responded by whipping his head towards him. His snapping mouth caught him, tearing a chunk of flesh from his arm.

'Motherfucker,' Chris shouted, dropping the drummer back onto the body of the twitching Mr Smart.

The instant Keith was back on the old man, he resumed chewing into his face.

The screaming continued as Chris fell backwards, holding his bleeding arm.

Keith lifted his head, hissing and spitting blood, as his purple eyes scanned the hall.

On seeing the blood-soaked face and gore filled mouth, everyone backed away, creating space between themselves and the horrors unfolding before them. No-one knew what to do, but they did know they wanted no part of it.

'Get him,' someone shouted, but no-one, including the members of the football team, and the remaining members of the band, acted upon the call to arms. Everyone was looking at each other, at the half-eaten body of Mr Smart, and at the bloody, crazed drummer.

'BRRRRRAAAAAAAIIINNNNNNSSSSSS!' Keith hissed again, spitting bits of Mr Sharp's face towards the crowd. He then stood shakily on his feet and turned a full three-hundred-and-sixty-degrees.

Jason tapped Brad on the shoulder and motioned towards the table, the one holding the huge punch bowl and the paper cups. He tipped his head, Brad got the gist of what he meant, and both boys moved into action. As Keith growled and hissed at everyone in the room, the two boys slowly made their way over.

'On three...' Jason whispered.

Brad nodded.

'One... two... three... NOW!'

The boys grabbed the table, lifted it without spilling the punch, and threw it at the growling thing that used to play drums. The throw was true, and it hit its target. It struck the boy-thing in the chest, knocking him over, while the bowl tipped, spilling its contents onto the floor.

The table trapped the drummer, holding him between it and the wall. But the surprise of the attack had not taken any of the fight out of the youth. He was still hissing and spitting, swiping his clawed hands towards anyone, and everyone, in the hall.

With a surge of energy and strength, the ex-drummer pushed the table away and lunged at the crowd who were gawping at what was unfolding. He grabbed a girl and knocked her to the floor. The ugly, gaping maw of his mouth was mere inches away from her face when Jason swung the heavy punchbowl.

The thud as it connected with the artist formerly known as Keith's head would have been comical if not for the grave seriousness of the situation. He crumpled, unceremoniously, onto the floor, away from the screaming girl, and onto his back, where he lay motionless. There was no more growling, no more screeching, and no more gnashing and swiping. Keith was dead.

'Oh shit, you killed him,' Bruce shouted over the resulting silence.

Jason and Brad turned to look at the guitarist in the stupid cloak. 'I... we... didn't mean to,' Jason stuttered.

'How the Hell are we going to finish the gig now?' Bruce continued, hobbling in his oversized boots towards the two boys. He swished his cloak over his shoulder, clenching his fists. He lost his footing for a moment as the stacked heels slipped on the spilled punch. There was a vague, vacant look in his eyes.

Brad shielded Jason from the approaching guitarist in the tight-fitting leotard, with his body. 'Look around you, dude. This gig's over. I don't know what's going on, but your buddy here just ate old Mr Smart. Jason took him out before he could do any more damage.'

'He was our driver, man,' Bruce shouted. 'How are we supposed to get away from this madness now?'

Brad could see the anxiety in the guitarist's eyes; a wildness about them. He could tell it was fear, but he thought it went deeper than that. Not the same fear you saw in other football players' eyes when you were bearing down on them on the field, no, this was real, life-or-death scenario fear. 'No-one's going anywhere,' he shouted. 'If there's more things like this out there, then we have to help our buddies, and we need to get the fricking police, and the ambulances, and maybe even the army, out here.'

Jason was back at the window, looking out. As he put his head to the glass, something hit it, scaring him into jumping back. 'Shit,' he shouted as he looked at the window and saw the blood-soaked jacket Razor had been wearing slide down the glass, leaving a bloody trail in its wake.

'Is that...?' Hank asked, putting his hand on Jason's shoulder.

'Razor's? Yes,' he replied, slowly.

Hank blessed himself with the sign of the cross. 'Oh, Holy mother of Jesus...' he whispered.

~~~~

In the confusion of Keith's attack, and with Jason diverting attention to the window, and what was happening outside, no-one noticed Mr Smart's body begin to twitch, or the wound on Chris's arm, where he had been bitten, begin to bubble and fester.

23.

THE EX-GIRLS DREW closer to the hissing and the screeching. The purple lights were everywhere now, staggering and shuffling towards the large building with the lights.

The cheerleaders never once broke formation, walking in a perfect triangle, each of them clicking their fingers in flawless rhythm with their steps.

A different kind of shouting had erupted for a few moments, these ones sounded human. As a collective, they knew the things they had been sent to clean up had claimed another human life. It disappointed them, but there was nothing they could do about it now.

The battle was coming, and they were ready for it. They had been given a mission, and they would do their utmost to fulfil it.

They were set to become Mutant Superhero Zombie Killing Cheerleaders!

24.

ROB WAS SURROUNDED. He'd run away from his best friend when he'd needed him the most, confirming what he'd known his whole life.

He was a coward.

He'd known this from a very early age. He had always been much bigger than the other kids in his class and had found it hard to make friends. He'd always been embarrassed by having to wear his father's cast-off clothes for school, as the shops didn't carry clothes that would fit him for his age. This was why he'd started to pick on the smaller kids. He thought that by hitting them, and stealing their lunch money, he would somehow be accepted by others. That he would be feared and respected, and maybe feel involved. He needed to show *himself* that he wasn't a coward. For a short while, he felt tough as he watched the smaller kids tremble in his presence.

That was before he met Jason and Razor.

They had both confronted him. Challenged him. Made him think about who he really was. Then they accepted him, became his friends, real friends. The first, and only ones, he'd ever had.

They persuaded him to join the football team. Due to his size, his popularity soared. He learned discipline, he learned how to control his anger, he became a team-player, but most of all, he learned how to control his cowardice.

Or so he had thought.

When he saw the *thing* dragging Razor out of the van, it opened a door that allowed the scaredy-cat Rob to come scurrying back through.

He left his friend, he had run away from him when he needed him most, and hid in the bushes, cowering like a kitten.

His plan was to make a break for it, to run and run and run, as far and as fast as he was able. This plan had been ruined by the number of purple eyed monsters shuffling around the parking lot. He thought he'd seen hundreds, maybe thousands, everywhere, all of them in various states of decay. They were hissing, screeching, and shambling. He'd heard Razor scream. It sounded like he was in agony, and then suddenly, he was silent. Rob feared the worst. Actually, he didn't *fear* the worst, he knew what had happened. *Exactly what the crazy drummer said about the girl,* he thought. *Eaten alive by the dead looking fucks.*

Screams were coming from the hall now. His stomach dropped at the sounds. They sounded male, followed by more male, and then a whole host of female. *What the Hell is going on in there?* He looked out from his hiding spot, but all he could see were monsters hobbling aimlessly about. He looked at the hall and saw that the doors were still closed; he couldn't fathom how the things could have gotten inside.

He cursed himself. He wanted to run for it, to get away, but the new, stronger part of him wanted to get into the hall, to try the phones to see if they were working, to call the police. He wanted this whole ordeal over with as soon as he could.

He closed his eyes.

All he could hear was the rain, the hissing, and shuffling of the monsters, and his own thoughts. *Come on, Rob, you can do this. You know you can. All you need to do is to get over to the door. It's not even a hundred yards away. You can run that in just over eleven seconds. You get in, you call the police, and then we get everyone out of there. Simple. Everyone is safe, and you're a hero! You get that? Don't you?*

He had it. He knew he could be a hero. He did have it in him. He took in a deep breath. 'One…' he whispered. 'Two, thr—'

Blue and red flashing lights, coupled with the welcoming sound of a siren, broke through the night.

It was a police siren!

He was saved.

He was going to live to be a coward another day.

He exhaled as deeply as he could and attempted to stand from his hiding place. That was when he noticed the monsters had also heard the sirens. Acting almost as one unit, they turned to see where the new wailing was coming from.

Rob watched as the car with the flashing lights on the roof pulled into the muddy parking lot, he saw the lights in the cabin come on, and he saw one of the men talking on a radio. The second one picked up a shotgun and checked it. He then put his hat on and opened the car door.

He wanted to run to them. He wanted nothing more than to be in the warm, dry safety of the back of that car.

He stood up and was about to shout, to call for help. With their badges and their guns, he knew he would be safe. It was a beautiful fantasy, only it was one that was ruined before it even started as one of the men climbed out of the car.

~~~~~

'All we have to do is check in, drive around the parking lot, make sure no ones smoking marijuana or performing lewd acts in their cars, and then we're out of there, back to the coffee shop. You good with that?' Sheriff Hanley asked, pulling the patrol car into the flooded parking lot.

'Ten-four that, Sheriff,' Deputy Pulis replied, leaning forwards to wipe the condensation from the windows with the sleeve of his beige uniform shirt. 'Although, I don't know how we're going to get to see any action with these windows how they are.'

'Oh, we'll see it,' the older man replied. 'If they're doing the nasty, the car will be rocking. If they're smoking, they'll have the windows down in the rain. Simple policing, son, simple policing.'

The young deputy raised his eyebrows and sat back into the passenger seat, nodding.

'Watch what happens when I do this…' The old man grinned as he flicked the sirens for a short burst.

Both men looked out of the windows. The older man was expecting movement, a lot of movement, from the parked cars and was more than a little disappointed when several, semi-naked college girls didn't jump from the vehicles, running into the bushes.

That was always his favourite part.

'Are you seeing what I'm seeing?' Pulis asked as he looked out of the window.

The older man leaned forwards and began to wipe at the condensation on his side. 'Well, I'll be darned. What the Hell is that?'

'I don't know, Sheriff, but there seems to be an awful lot of them.'

Glowing purple lights were floating around in the darkness. There were also other movements around the purple lights, as if people were carrying them around.

'They seem to be attracted to the car, sir,' Pulis said as he retrieved the shotgun from between the seats.

'I'd say you're right, kid. You go and take a look. I'll radio it in.'

'Ten-four that.' Pulis reached into the footwell of the passenger seat and picked up his hat. Even if it hadn't been protocol to be wearing it as he exited the vehicle, the way the rain was pouring down hard, he didn't want to ruin the haircut he'd had today. Missy Walker, his girlfriend, deserved the best, and that meant a haircut, a shave, and maybe even a bath.

As he opened the door to climb out of the car, he heard Sheriff Hanley calling it in.

'This is Car One to base, can you hear me?'

'Car One, you're coming through loud and clear, Dan,' the electronic voice replied from the speakers.

'How many times to do I have to tell you? Don't call me Dan on the radio! It's Sheriff Hanley when we're in the office.'

'But you're not in the office, sir,' the barely recognisable female voice replied.

The old man shook his head and took his finger off the send button on the side of the handpiece. 'Idiot!' he mumbled underneath his breath. 'Why do I surround myself with idiots?' He put his finger back on the button and spoke into the handset. 'Just take the report, will you? We're at Oldman's Barn where the high-school party is happening. We're doing a once around. There's no music coming from inside the barn, and there are several purple lights floating around. Pulis is just about to investigate... OH HOLY SWEET MOTHER OF OUR LORD JESUS CHRIST AND THE ORPHANS OF HEAVEN!' he screamed.

~~~~

Rob watched from the bushes, thanking the Lord that he hadn't shouted out to alert the deputies to his presence. He watched as the younger man put his hat on and stepped out of the car.

That was the exact point that everything went to Hell in a handcart.

The young man shifted his hat to combat the rain that was pouring down on him. He was holding the pump action shotgun in his other hand.

The poor guy never had a chance.

From out of nowhere, the glowing purple lights, and the monsters they were glowing from, descended on the hapless deputy.

Rob wanted to help; he wanted to rush out and distract the monsters from the young man; he wanted to go at them as if they were a football defensive line and take them all out. But unfortunately, his inner chicken wouldn't let him move. Even more unfortunately, his inner chicken also turned out to be a voyeur. He couldn't take his eyes off what was happening only a few yards away.

The deputy didn't even see the first wave coming. As he adjusted the hat on his head, the first one, the one wearing the pink panties on its head, snuck up on his blind spot. It was surprisingly slick and silent for something so awkward and cumbersome. It crept up from the side and went straight for the unsuspecting man's neck.

'BRRRRRAAAAAAIIINNNNNNSSSSSS!' it hissed.

The deputy turned toward the sound, straight into the thing's bite, and in one snap of its dirty, strong jaws, it bit his nose clean off.

'WHAT THE…' he shouted before dropping his gun and raising both hands to his face. Instantly, another thing was on him from the other side. This one was also snapping at his face. Rob watched as an ear was bitten off. The arc of blood sprayed over the window of the patrol car behind him.

A third monster took its assault straight on. As the young man thrashed his head back in agony from the loss of his ear, and nose, the thing missed and ended up falling on him, wrapping its arms around his neck. This caused the first monster—the one with the pink panties still wrapped around its neck, like a grotesque fashion statement—to lunge and bite the arm of the third monster.

A thick chunk of rotten flesh came off into its mouth. It didn't even flinch. It just spat out the offending morsel, as if it was not to its taste, wiped its mouth, and lunged back in for another bite.

The incapacitated deputy fell back against the car as the three things bit, snapped, and tore at him. Most of his face had already been eaten away, along with chunks of his shoulder and chest.

'BRRRRRAAAAAAIIINNNNNNSSSSSS!' they hissed.

Get out of the car, Rob willed the older man who was still sitting in the driver's side, still holding the handpiece of the radio. *Get out of the car and kill those fucking things!*

To his dismay, Rob felt something warm begin to trickle down his leg. In a panic, he looked and was relieved to find that the warmth was just him pissing his pants. *Thank God for that,* he thought. *For a moment there, I thought it was blood!*

~~~~

'Shit… Holy fuck! Brenda… Brenda, can you hear me?'

'Loud and clear, Dan… I mean Sheriff. What's happening?'

'Shut up and listen to me. They've got Pulis!'

'Shut up? Who's got Pulis?'

'Fuck, they're tearing him apart. Get re-enforcements out here, immediately. Tell them to load up on weapons. Holy fuck, were going to need them.'

'Dan, you're scaring me,' the electronic voice came back from the radio. It sounded high-pitched and terrified.

'Get them to open the special cabinet, the emergency cabinet. Do you hear me? Tell them to bring everything they can. Shit, get the Fire

Department out here as well. Load them up with weapons. The National Guard too. Hell, get the Army. There's thousands of them!'

'Sir, Dan... Sheriff! What are you talking about?'

'Get them out here. NOW! Oldman's barn out on Cemetery Road. I need men here and I need them here with the extra weapons. Can you do that, you numbskull?' Sheriff Hanley shouted down the handpiece.

'Yes... yes, I can,' came the shouted, panicked, reply.

'Then fucking DO it then. Remember, *the special cabinet.* Hanley OUT!'

The old man watched as his best friend's son, his godson, his ward, fell back against the car as the blood spurting from the wounds on his face splattered and covered the windows. 'All right, you motherfuckers...' he snapped, pulling his gun out of his holster, and checking it for bullets. 'Let's see how you like this shit!'

~~~~

Rob's vision blurred as tears began to well in his eyes. He watched the young deputy fall to the ground. He didn't want to continue watching as the group of ghouls dropped with him, but his voyeur coward did. Mercifully, when the ghouls dropped with the deputy, they fell out of his line of sight. But they weren't out of his hearing range. He could hear the whimpering cries for help from the deputy, cutting through the rain, and the salivating, slobbering chomps and snaps of whatever the things were eating him.

Another noise joined the deathly chorus of the night. It was a human noise and one that brought a level of hope back into Rob's heart. 'All right, you motherfuckers,' an old man shouted over the constant roar of the rain. 'How about eating some of this?'

Rob wiped his eyes just in time to see the sheriff put the muzzle of his service revolver into the face of one of the advancing monsters. He didn't spare a moment in pulling the trigger.

The gun's report was muffled, both by the rain and the proximity to the hungry beast's face, but it was loud enough to gain the attention of several the other things milling around the parking lot. Working as if serviced by a hive mind, the rotten, ugly faces turned towards the gun shot.

Rob watched the vile creature drop to the floor with a spray of purple gore erupting from the back of its head. He clenched his fists together and punched the air. 'Yes,' he hissed. 'Take that, you brain-eating turd,' he hooted.

The other things began to advance on the location of the shot. 'BRRRRRAAAAAAIIINNNNNNSSSSSS!' they all hissed.

Rob had faith in the Sheriff.

He watched as the old man put his gun into the face of another ghoul and pulled the trigger. Once again, a muffled report heralded a volcanic eruption of rotting brain matter from the back of its head.

Two more shots ensued, and two more dead fucks dropped to the ground. This gave Rob all the impetus he needed to leave his hiding space. 'Sheriff,' he shouted. 'I'm with you!' He saw the shotgun that the Deputy had dropped lying in a puddle next to the writhing mass of things that were still eating him. He ignored the nastiness and concentrated on the weapon that was no more than thirty yards away.

~~~~

Sheriff Hanley, busily dispatching the advancing hoard, was momentarily distracted by a large, shouting thing lumbering out of the bushes. It was rushing towards him. He brought his gun around and aimed it at the hulk in the tuxedo jacket. Without a second thought, he fired. His aim was true, and he took the enormous, rushing beast down with one shot.

Satisfied that he'd bagged the big one, he took another shot, dropping another monster, before taking a moment to reload his revolver, something he could do in his sleep from years of practice, and continued to dispatch the others that were shuffling towards him.

~~~~~

A small red hole appeared in Rob's forehead.

His excited face changed into one of confusion. His legs, caught in motion, continued as his head was thrown backwards by the impact of whatever it was that had hit him. As he fell, his thoughts became wild and erratic. They began to merge. *Wow, I really need to learn how to cook mom's lasagne, I'm going to need it for the Spanish test on Tuesday.* As his feet stopped working, he looked down at all four of them and grinned. *Winged feet, just like an octopus!*

The floor then rose upwards to meet him. It was a strange phenomenon because he knew that up was down and down was up... and the puddle that was now caressing his face shouldn't be vertical.

BANG!

The report was delayed, in what was left of his head anyway.

His neck was hurting, as was the sharp pain in the centre of his head. He wanted to lift his hand to swat whatever insect was annoying him, the one that was trying to burrow into his head, but his limbs were doing their own thing.

That thing they were doing was twitching.

The night became brighter, and the rain became translucent. Then he saw the face of an angel, it was leaning into him and smiling.

That's one ugly fucking angel, he laughed.

This was his last thought before darkness consumed him and his strange thoughts disappeared, forever.

~~~~

The sheriff only realised what he'd done after he had taken out more of the beasts.

He looked over at the hulking great mass of tuxedo jacket lying on the ground and reality hit him. The bulk lying in the bloody puddle wasn't one of the beasts.

It was a boy.

A human boy.

His mouth dropped as he realised that the kid must have been hiding in the woods, obviously scared out of his mind, and had been running towards him for help. 'I… I couldn't tell…' he stammered as he watched the boy twitching on the ground. There was a goofy grin on his young face, and a huge gaping hole at the back of his head, as he lay on the muddy ground of the parking lot. 'No,' he whispered, as the darkness pouring from the hole spread into the otherwise muddy puddle.

The old man, no longer holding his gun in the air, with his eyes transfixed on the bleeding body of the boy in the water, didn't see the pack of ghouls approach.

He didn't care anymore anyway.

I've done a bad thing, he thought as the first monster bit into his neck. The second was on him in a flash, as were the third and fourth.

Five sets of strong teeth tore into his soft flesh, clawing him, tearing at the meat of his body, dragging him down into the mud. The agony he felt as he was slowly devoured alive was second only to the pain of knowing what he'd done. He'd taken the life of a young man, an innocent youth. As he succumbed to the monsters, he never once took his eyes from the body in the puddle, the one being devoured by a rotten, reanimated corpse.

He fired the gun once more. The bullet landed harmlessly in the mud, causing a small splash.

25.

THE RAIN SHOULD have been soaking the cheerleaders, to the bones; their hair should have been plastered against their heads, their cheerleader jerseys should have been clinging to every curve of their young, athletic bodies, their short skirts should have been ruined with the rain and the mud.

But they weren't.

They stepped in rhythm, clicking their fingers with every step they took, as dry and as clean as if they had stayed inside the whole night. The leader, the one with the large afro hairdo, stopped as two loud bangs rang out into the night. She held up her hand. As if working as a machine, the rest of them stopped too. As one, they lifted their heads into the air, sensing where the continued reports were come from.

As an eighth report rang through the night, the leader clicked her fingers again. The others clicked their fingers in response.

Then they continued their march in close formation.

26.

'THE COPS ARE here,' Jason shouted as he looked through the window at the blue and red flashes illuminating the dreary night. He also noted that the purple glowing eyes seemed to be everywhere now.

'Thank God for that,' Hank replied, sidling up next to him to look out of the window. 'That singer dude isn't looking so good,' he whispered, putting his head against the cool, wet glass.

Jason turned to look. The singer was with Brad, moving the body of the drummer to the other side of the room, next to the body of Mr Smart. Jason was relieved that someone had the good sense to cover the poor man's corpse with a coat.

Geoff stood up and held onto his lower back, as if moving the body had taken it out of him. His face was pale, but was flushed in his cheeks, and he looked like he was sweating, too much.

'Do you think...?' Hank asked.

He didn't need to finish his question as Jason already knew what it was going to be. 'I don't know,' he interrupted. 'But if he's going to change into one of those things, then we need to be ready for it. We can't have another incident like Mr Smart.'

'Hey, everyone,' someone else from one of the other windows shouted back into the hall. 'The cops are here. It's all going to be OK!'

A cheer erupted, and a few of the others ran to the windows to see the blue and red lights, just in time to hear the wail of the sirens. 'Do they really want to be doing that?' One of the girls asked as she looked out into the night.

'Yeah, of course they do,' a boy standing next to her replied. 'It'll show them assholes out there that you can't mess around scaring people. Someone's in big trouble now.' He was smiling as he turned back to look out the window.

The smile didn't last long.

'Oh shit, what's he doing?' Jason shouted as he watched the Deputy get out of the car and adjust his hat. 'Look out, man. LOOK OUT!'

A strange, shocked silence fell over the hall.

'What's happening?' Geoff shouted, after placing a coat over the body of Keith, covering his face.

No-one replied.

'What's happening?' he called again, making his way over to the window, wiping his friend's blood from his hands, onto his trousers.

Jason turned to look at him, his face was devoid of humour. He shook his head, slowly.

Geoff's eyes narrowed as he pushed past Jason to look out of the window himself.

Outside, the young deputy was on the floor with three things writhing on top of him like some weird, grotesque porn film. Then the porn film got weirder as the sheriff exited the car.

There was a bang, and everyone in the hall, including Geoff and Jason, either screamed or jumped. Both boys looked back out the window and watched as the sheriff put the muzzle of his gun to the head of one of the shuffling things and pulled the trigger. There was another muffled bang, and the thing fell to the floor, dead, or at least deader than it already was.

136

Another cheer tore through the room.

We're saved, Jason thought as a smile broke on his face.

A slurry of gunshots could be heard, each of them was followed with a cheer.

'Everyone, we need to get that door open. The sheriff is outside, and he'll be in here any minute,' Jason shouted. His heart was beating fast, but there was a lightness to him now, as he thought they might just make it through the night.

This thought came to him before the fifth gunshot tore through the night. It was closely followed by a scream.

At first, Jason thought it was coming from outside, and his heart sank in his chest again. *No,* he thought. *Not when we're this close!*

It took a moment for him to realise that the scream was coming from inside the hall. His first instinct made him look over towards the dead bodies in the corner. He didn't trust them, not after what he'd seen happen to Keith. When he saw they weren't moving, he looked at Chris, who was leaning against the wall, looking deathly pale, and holding onto his arm.

The scream was nothing to do with him either.

Then he heard a word. It came from within the room, and it made him feel cold. The numbness coursed through him like when he ate freezing cold ice cream, and he could feel the icy goodness travel along all the tubes in his body.

The word that was shouted was...

'ROB!'

Rob? he thought.

Then the screams turned into cries.

Rob, he thought again.

The cries turned to sobs.

Jason looked around. The kids who had been looking out of the windows were turning away, facing back into the hall. They were either crying or had vacant, shocked, looks in their eyes. He searched for Hank, or Kevin. When he saw them, he wished he hadn't. They looked worse than Chris from the band.

'What's happening?' he asked. The question was to no-one, but also to everyone. 'What the fuck's happening?' he asked again.

'Rob,' Kevin said and dropped his head.

Jason pushed past him and ran to the window. At first, he thought he couldn't see anything because of the condensation on the windows, then he thought it was because of the glare of the lights behind him, he also thought that it might be to do with the rain that was teeming down out there. But it was none of them. It was a moment before he realised it was because of the tears that were building up in his eyes. Tears, because somehow, he knew what he was going to see out of this window.

To his utter horror, he was right.

His eyes were drawn to the sheriff being dragged down onto the muddy ground by three, four, or maybe even five, of the horrors out there. The terror in this scene was too much for him to take but yet he still had to drag his eyes away.

Then, once again, he wished he hadn't.

His worst nightmare had come true.

It was Rob!

He was lying on the floor, his face in a deep puddle, while one of the things with purple eyes feasted upon his head.

Slowly, he turned away, he couldn't watch anymore.

Now they were well and truly on their own.

27.

'HE SAID TO open the special cupboard and to call the Fire Department, the National Guard, *and* the Army. I don't know what to do!' The young woman sitting by the radio was gripping the microphone like it was poisonous snake that might bite her at any given moment. Her back was to the radio as she addressed the small room that was filled with tan-uniformed cops.

A large man, who was barely containing his massive belly within the confines of his shirt, looked at the scared girl. 'Let me clarify that, little lady! He said the *special cupboard*?'

'Those were the exact words he used, yes. He mentioned the Fire Department and the National Guard too.' The girl was shifting in her seat, as her wide eyes regarded all the men looking at her. *Why did I volunteer tonight?* she thought. *I could have been at the dance with my little sister, watching the band.*

The big man's lip twitched, making his thin ginger moustache dance on his face. He looked around at the others in the room. There were five of them in total, and they were all looking at him. He nodded, grinding his teeth. He then held out his hand towards Laurie. 'Give me the radio,' he ordered in a soft, but authoritative, voice. With an air of relief, she handed the microphone over to the big man.

'Dan… Dan, this is Dave. Can you hear me, boss?' He let go of the button, anticipating a swift response.

Nothing was forthcoming.

'Sheriff, can you hear me? Come in, this is Deputy Dave! Big Dave Coleman.' Once again, he released the button, again to no avail. All that came through the speakers was static.

He looked around the room. Everyone had stopped what they were doing and were looking back at him. He swallowed hard as his eyes joined the dancing that his moustache had started. 'OK, here's what we're going to do. We're going to get the day shift in, get the volunteer fire department in too, tell them it's overtime, tell them I don't care if they're drunk or whatever, I want them here in ten minutes. Tell them it's Priority One, they'll know what that means. Get onto it right now!'

Laurie nodded and turned around, spinning the rolodex on her desk.

~~~~

Twenty minutes later, the already crowded room at the Sheriff's Office was full. There were fifteen men, plus 'Big' Dave Coleman. Some of them were wearing sheriff deputy uniforms, some were wearing fire department uniforms, the rest were dressed in civilian clothing, mostly plaid or checked shirts and overcoats.

All of them were smoking.

'OK, men, the situation is dire. Twenty minutes ago, we received a message from Sheriff Dan, requesting help, but a rather specific kind of help. He mentioned…' he paused then, more for dramatic effect than anything else, as his eyes roamed around the room, taking special care to meet with *everyone's* gaze. '…the special cupboard!'

The electricity in the room began to tingle at the mention of *the special cupboard.* Everyone began to either cough, or shuffle. If there had been a temperature gauge in the room, it would have been climbing to fever point.

'We've had no further contact from either Sheriff Dan or Deputy Pulis, so we're going to assume the worst.' Once again, this caused more coughing and shuffling. 'And, we're going to do what he requested. We're going to open *the special cupboard.*'

He strode slowly, but purposefully, around to the back of the room, aware of the fifteen sets of eyes watching his every move. As he reached the large filing cabinet he stopped. He looked at it for a few moments, there was reverence in his gaze.

With a sigh, he rolled up his shirt sleeves and bent his knees. His face flushed red as he grabbed the set of drawers and pulled them. He huffed and puffed as he slowly shifted the cabinet away from the back wall. He spared a glance towards the men, hoping for an offer of help; but none was forthcoming, so he continued to struggle on his own.

When it was moved just enough for him to reach his bulk behind it, he did so. His face was turning even redder, almost purple, as he reached around the back of the cabinet. Still, everyone in the room watched him, all of them smoking, none of them speaking.

His fat fingers fumbled around until they made contact with what he was looking for. A small keyring, taped to the back of the cabinet. He reached for it, three times, twice the metal ring slipped from his moist fingers, before finally finding purchase. He ripped the adhesive strip from the metal, with a grunt, and a sigh. He corrected himself, swallowing, and waiting for the room to stop spinning, before straightening his tight-fitting shirt back over the pink of his exposed belly.

He noticed with some distain that in his mission to retrieve the key, there had been at least two casualties. Shirt buttons. He fixed himself as best as he could and continued to move the cabinet back into place. Once again, with no help from anyone else.

Once the cabinet was back in place, he took a few moments to allow the stars that were dancing around his peripheral vision to dissolve, and for his blood pressure to return to some semblance of normal. Once this had passed, he took the key and sat at Sheriff Dan's desk, doing so with an audible sigh, and a scream of resistance from the seat. He fumbled around, trying to fit the single silver key into the top drawer. He looked up at the fifteen spectators who were all leaning towards him, in rapture at what he was doing. He offered them a small smile, more from embarrassment than anything else, as he wiped at the sweat on his top lip that was tickling his moustache. The key didn't fit. He then tried the second drawer; once again, there was no luck. Rolling his eyes, and sweating profusely by now, he attempted the key into the top drawer of the other side, and to his obvious relief, it opened.

As it did, his audience breathed a collective sigh of relief, and all sat back again.

He opened the draw, only to find a single scrap of paper. On the paper were written four numbers in Sheriff Dan's handwriting.

The number was four sixes.

He took the paper out of the drawer and proceeded towards the locked door in the corner of the room. Again, fifteen pairs of eyes followed him. Without saying a word, he grasped the combination lock and looked at the numbers on it. The four small metal dials were all set to zero. With a small glance at the collection of deputies looking back at him, he proceeded to move the dials, one by one, to the six setting. He took a deep breath and pulled at the lock.

It didn't move.

He cleared his throat and looked at the lock again. He noticed that the second dial was only halfway between the five and the six. He corrected it and gave the lock another tug.

There was still no movement.

With his heartbeat pounding in his ears, he looked again at the piece of paper in his hands. There were four sixes. He looked at the lock to make sure that he had selected four sixes.

He had.

What the Hell is going on here? he thought, offering a small smile to his audience.

He looked at the paper again and noticed little lines underneath the sixes. He then turned the paper upside down and watched as the four sixes became four nines.

His sweating fingers spun the dials to get all the nines in line. He took another breath, closed his eyes, said a silent prayer to whatever saint was in charge of opening combination locks in front of an audience, and pulled it.

He lifted his head and breathed deeply as the lock snapped open.

'OK, gents,' he said when he had removed the lock from the door. 'Gather round while I open *the special cupboard.*'

The whole room, including the young woman on the dispatch radio, shuffled forward as Deputy 'Big Dave' Coleman opened the door.

28.

THE MAIN DOOR was blocked with piled furniture, tables, and chairs. Jason had sent some of the others around the hall to check out, and block, any other possible ways into the barn.

'The only way in or out of this building now is through these windows,' Kevin reported when he returned from the scouting expedition. 'I'd say we're safe, for now, but I don't think we can stay here too long. There's plenty of water but not a lot of food.'

Jason looked around at the rest of the revellers in the barn. They looked tired, shocked, and more than a little scared. Most of them were healthy, with the obvious exceptions of the two dead bodies, and Chris, who had been bitten. 'I think we need to keep an eye on that one,' he whispered to Kevin, indicating Chris. 'I'm not liking that purple tinge in his eyes, not one bit.'

Kevin nodded as he looked over, catching the eyes of Bruce, the guitarist.

'What are you looking at?' Bruce sneered, his brow ruffling as his eyebrows knitted closer together.

Kevin quickly looked away.

'You better look away, little boy,' he continued. 'My friend here is OK. He's just tired from an over excitable night. Right, Chris?' He turned towards the injured bass player and nudged him. 'Aren't you? All right? Tell him, man. Tell him you're all right!'

As if on cue, Chris began to heave.

Bruce saw what was happening and stepped away, remembering what happened when Keith started. 'Chris, man, watch the cloak!' he shouted swishing the material away from the sluice of vomit. Once he was out of its path and had checked the cloth for any stray bits of puke, he looked at his friend. His eyes widened. 'You *are* all right, aren't you?' he asked, his voice shaking.

Chris didn't answer. He just heaved again.

'What's happening over there?' Jason shouted.

Bruce stepped in front of his friend, holding out his cloak to shield him from Jason's view. 'Erm, nothing. Nothing's happening. We're all good over here. How are you?'

The sounds of Chris retching were getting louder.

'Man, eew. That guy has just heaved a fucking lung,' someone shouted from behind him. Bruce closed his eyes and gritted his teeth.

'What?' Jason shouted and bolted across the hall. He pushed Bruce out of the way and stared at Chris.

He was deathly pale. There were dark purple rings around his eyes, giving him a panda bear look, only nowhere near as cute. His lips were purple and there was a sheen of sweat over all the exposed areas of his skin. His T-shirt was covered in blood and vomit from Keith and new blood and vomit from himself.

'No way,' Jason muttered. 'We've got to get him out of here.' He stood up and looked at the guitarist in the stupid cloak, who stared back at him with eyes that were pleading for help, but his mouth was stubborn.

'He's going nowhere. He'll be OK. I think he just drank a bad bottle of beer, or something,' Bruce argued as he guarded his friend. Jason could see that all he wanted to do was protect his friend, but that his loyalty was overshadowed by his desire to get as far away from him as was humanly possible, which, in this hall was not far away at all.

'There's no bad bottle of beer that would do that to someone,' Jason hissed. 'That's the exact same look I saw on your drummer's face, right before he bit into Mr Smart.'

Bruce shook his head as Geoff made his way over. 'What are you saying? Are you telling me Chris is going to change into one of those... things?' he asked.

Jason shrugged. He didn't know, he didn't have a clue, but he didn't want to be stuck in this hall if it *did* happen. 'I don't know anything, man,' he confessed. 'But I do know he needs medical attention. Can you get him into the back and see if there's anything we can use to help him?' Jason had a hunch there wasn't anything anywhere that could help the poor bass player now, but he wanted him out of the hall and away from the others.

Geoff, who had been watching the argument from the sides, agreed. 'The way it is in here, after the old man got it, I think these kids are just about ready to spring him anyway. Give me a hand, Bruce.' The two band members reluctantly took Chris by the arms and led him away across the hall, towards the back of the stage.

As Jason watched them go, he put his head in his hands and exhaled. *Why me?* he thought. *Why do I have to get stuck with being in charge? Where the Hell are Turnbull and Wellborn?* Even though he had a good idea where they were, he didn't want to give it a voice. He turned back to the window, looking at the faces of the other students, who were looking back at him for something. Guidance? Instruction? He didn't know. All he knew was that he didn't want the responsibility for their survival. However, he *was* determined not to lose anyone else tonight.

29.

THE BARN WAS dead ahead. The lights from the large building had attracted the hordes and they were currently milling around outside of it. There could have been a hundred of them, there could have been a thousand, it was impossible to tell due to their staggered, slow, but constant, movements.

The six girls were almost there. They had made their way along Cemetery Road, past the graveyard where these things had originated.

The rain had not tainted them. The mud had not sullied them. They moved as one unit, with one objective: to get to the barn as soon as they could.

The time they had spent submerged in the purple mud had changed them. They no longer cared about makeup, or their outfits, or the boys inside the barn. They didn't care about pyramids, or that the Lions had won the district cup and that this night was their celebration.

Their brains worked on a different level now.

They had a mission, and it was imperative they didn't fail.

Each of them had been given a gift.

Each of them knew how to use their gift.

Each of them would complete their mission using the gifts they had been so graciously given.

The monsters that had once been long dead humans didn't have any idea the Mutant Superhero Zombie Killing Disco Cheerleaders were on their way.

But they soon would!

30.

THE SIRENS WAILED through the rainy night. There were more of them this time. Their out of time song and their blue and red flashing lights were sending a message to all who heard, or saw, them. That message was, 'You don't fuck with us tonight. We're on a mission.'

Four patrol cars, each with four men inside, all loaded up with special equipment from the special cupboard, splashed down the flooded back roads of Kearney.

'I wish this rain would quit,' the driver of the first car moaned as he leaned forward to look out the windshield. 'I can't see a goddam thing on the road.'

'Just keep driving, you big pussy,' Deputy Dave Coleman quipped from the passenger seat. 'We're nearly there.'

As the four cars whipped down Cemetery Road, creating tidal waves of brown, muddy water in the night, their sirens caught the attention of the monsters currently besieging the barn.

'BRRRRRAAAAAAIIINNNNNNSSSSSS!' they all hissed in anticipation of their fast-food delivery.

'Step on it, boy,' Deputy Dave Colman ordered. 'The sheriff is out there somewhere, and I intend to find him and make sure everything is OK.'

The driver turned towards the big deputy with a look that asked, 'who died and put you in charge?' He very nearly said it out loud before realising where they were and what they were doing with the special equipment. So, he swallowed his words and turned back to the fast-running river that used to be Cemetery Road.

The other cars were close behind. Deputy Dave Coleman turned back to look at the two men sitting in the back. 'Can one of you boys wipe the back window, please? I can't see a thing back there.'

One of the men turned and wiped at the condensation.

Deputy Dave Coleman picked up the radio from the dash and pressed the small button on the side. This called all the other cars and the dispatcher back in the office.

'OK, can you all hear me?' he asked.

There was a small chorus of acknowledgments.

'Good. We're nearly there, and I'm not one hundred percent sure what we're going to find. But I do know this. The Sheriff asked us to get the special equipment for a reason, so I'm expecting it to be bad. I want you all to be ready for anything. You got that?'

Again, there was another round of acknowledgements.

'Good, were coming up on Oldman's Barn in a minute or so. We'll form a protective circle with the cars as much as we can in the parking lot, then we'll get out and control the situation. I can't see anyone giving us any trouble with our special equipment. Is everyone clear on that?'

The chorus told him that they were.

'Good, let's do this for Sheriff Hanley and Deputy Pulis.' He put the hand piece back in its cradle and turned to look at the men in the back. 'Everyone ready?' he asked. A small smile spread across his face as the two men in the back picked up their Uzi submachine guns and checked the large magazines protruding from the bottom.

'Locked and loaded, sir,' one of the young deputies replied.

'I can't see much shit going down here tonight, sir,' the second one replied. 'Not with these bad boys at our disposal.'

'Well, let's just hope it doesn't come to us using them,' Deputy Dave Coleman replied, not really convincing himself that he meant it. He picked up the submachine gun he had on his lap and checked the magazine. If he was being truthful, he was itching to use this bad boy.

~~~~

'Help... help me. Get me the fuck out of here right now!' The shouts were coming from the green room at the back of the stage area, the location where Jason had asked the band members to take Chris and the two dead bodies. The door banged and rattled in its frame as if it was being violently attacked from the other side.

That door's locked on the inside, Jason thought as he watched in horror as it thrashed. There were screams and groans and the occasional wet ripping sound. 'HELP!'

'It's locked from the inside,' Jason shouted through the door to whoever was shouting from inside. It must have been Geoff, or Bruce, the other two in there, Keith and Mr Smart, were dead. 'It's locked from your side,' he shouted again.

More screams and bangs came from behind the door. Jason put his hand on the handle and gave it a little tug. It was definitely locked. A blood curdling scream emitted from the other side of the wood, and Jason stepped back, suddenly glad there was the physical barrier between him and whatever was in there. Another shout rang out, and he stepped even further away from the door and whatever was happening behind it.

'Hey, Jason, get out here, man. More cops have turned up,' someone shouted from the main hall. The screams and thumps from behind the door had stopped, and before he turned away to see who was shouting to him, he spared one final glance back at the door handle.

The wood thumped once again as he headed away towards the hall, making his exit just that little bit quicker.

'Look, there's four cars this time. There's no way those crazy things out there will be able to get all of them.' It was Kevin who was shouting as he pulled Jason closer to the window.

Still feeling guilty for not doing more at the door to the changing room, Jason put his head to the window as the cars began to angle themselves into the parking lot. They were attempting to park in a circle, obviously for safety. But the other cars already parked stopped them from doing it correctly.

He wanted to feel relieved. He wanted to feel saved, safe; but he couldn't feel anything. He'd seen too much tonight. He thought about what was happening, and where Suzi was in all of this? He hoped she was alive and well, and many, many miles away from the purple eyed monsters who seemed to be eating everyone and anyone they could get their hands on.

'They've got Uzis!' someone shouted. He could tell that the person shouting was trying to sound triumphant, maybe even jubilant. But to Jason, it felt a little too empty.

He put his head back onto the windowpane in time to see the deputies climbing out of the cars. All of them holding submachine guns, some of them were wearing padding on their arms and legs. To him, they looked ill-prepared for what they were about to face. He felt an arm on his shoulder, and he turned to see Brad smiling at him.

'We're safe now, dude,' he grinned.

Jason tried to return the smile and found he couldn't. 'Let's hope so,' he murmured.

~~~~

'OK, men, lock and load. Let's see what all this shit is about,' Deputy Dave Coleman gushed as he checked his gun for the fifth time. He loved the way the heavy piece felt in his hands.

'This is the best I can do, Dave. I don't think we're going to get a full circle,' the driver, Deputy Brian Jones, said as he picked up his own gun and checked it.

'It'll do, Jonesy,' he replied, fixing his hat, and getting ready to leave the dry car and go forth into the pouring rain. 'Now let's go and find our men.' He got out of the car and made his way over to the small huddle of men, who were already soaking wet. They were all checking their guns. 'OK, guys, Sheriff Hanley is out here somewhere, as is Pulis. Our job is to find them and see what the hell is going on around here.'

'Dave,' one of the other Deputies shouted over the roar of the rain. 'Look over there, in the window.'

The deputies turned towards the large barn where they knew the party was being held. 'Are those kids waving at us?' Dave asked.

'I think they are,' Jones replied waving back at them.

'Come on now, we don't have time for frolicking with school kids. We've got a job to do. HOLY MOLY!' he shouted as he looked away from the barn.

Alerted by his shout, the other men in the cold, wet night looked over to what he was gawping at.

An entire crew of motley looking, dishevelled... *things,* were shuffling towards them. 'What the fuck have they come as?' he shouted. Then he turned towards his men, all of whom were gawping as he was. 'When is Halloween?'

One of the deputies, Alan Borrowdale, shook his head and stepped back, away from the approaching horde. 'N-not until October,' he stuttered. He continued to step away until he was right at the back of the crowd of spooked cops. He continued backing off while automatically checking his Uzi. He didn't notice that he was backing out of the relative

153

safety of the ring of lights formed by the patrol cars. His mind was too focused on the *things* that were lurching towards them behind the bright lights; the *things* that were making the growling and the mewling noises; the *things* with the glowing purple eyes.

He was far too busy in this train of thought to notice that the same *things* were also behind him.

As his nervous fingers fiddled with the submachine gun, something cold and strong grabbed him from behind. Every part of his body froze, except for one. Unfortunately for Deputy McDonald, who was standing in front of him, the one part that didn't freeze was his trigger finger. He had already released the safety on the weapon, and as his finger went into spasm, it tightened on the small metal trigger.

The gun that Deputy Borrowdale was holding was an Uzi.

Uzis are nearly twenty-five inches long with a barrel length of just over ten inches. Its effective range is around two-hundred and eighteen yards, and it can fire a burst of up to six-hundred rounds per minute.

Regrettably, for Deputy McDonald, Alan Borrowdale's finger was on the trigger for about ten seconds, resulting in the full capacity of 25 high speed rounds pumping into his body, as the unfortunate man was well within the weapon's effective range.

All the others ducked, throwing themselves to the ground at the reports from the submachine gun. Each deputy, Big Dave included, were holding onto their hats.

'Holy Fuck, Alan! What are you doing?' Coleman screamed as his face hit the freezing mud that was the ground of the parking lot. He looked up, just in time, to watch Jim McDonald fall to the floor in a bloody, bullet-hole-riddled mess.

The scream he heard hadn't come from the stricken deputy. It had originated from the direction of the gunfire. Dave Coleman thought it might have been Alan Borrowdale screaming in fear, and revulsion, at what he'd just done, but something about it didn't sound like remorse.

It sounded like pain.

Intense pain.

He was right. It was too painful for Deputy 'Big Dave' Coleman to watch.

So, he didn't.

As he shifted his glance from Jim on the floor towards Alan who had shot him, he forgot all about the mission. He forgot why they were here, he forgot where they were, and he forgot who he was with. All that consumed him was seeing a man he knew, a man he had worked with and respected, riddled with bullets, lying in a dirty puddle, as his life flowed out of him in red rivulets.

He shifted his gaze and watched as the man, Borrowdale, the one who had fired the gun that killed his friend, having his throat torn out by something, or someone, behind him. The thing that was attacking him was wearing a sheriff's hat and what looked like the remnants of a county uniform, one that was ripped, soaking wet, and covered in blood.

He recognised the attacker.

He watched as his boss, Sheriff Hanley, bit into the neck of the screaming deputy. He saw the slow-motion, arterial spray from the wound arching through the night air as his friend's teeth made short work of the man's carotid artery. This sight brought everything back to him. Suddenly, he knew where he was, why he was here, and more importantly, he knew who he was here with.

He turned away from his colleague being eaten alive. 'Holy fuck,' he whispered to himself, hoping none of the other men heard him. He averted his gaze down to the submachine gun in his hands and gritted his teeth. *No-one else is getting eaten tonight,* he thought. *Not on my watch!* With a well-trained hand, he flicked the safety off, and he turned back towards the thing that had taken a chomp out of Alan Borrowdale.

The ex-sheriff's blood smeared face regarded him. The purple fire in the dark recesses of his eyeholes glowed brighter, just for a moment, before it dropped the lifeless body of Alan and came at him.

Deputy Colman's heart thumped in his chest. His knees went weak, and his head began to swim. He bit down on his lip, hard enough to draw blood, and the world that was currently swimming around him, began to knit back together.

The thing that had eaten Alan wasn't on its own. It had friends, lots of them. They were surrounding him and his men, and if he had to guess he'd say that there were hundreds of them, all stinking, growling, and glowing.

'BRRRRRAAAAAAIIINNNNNNSSSSSS!' he heard them hiss and spit.

The rest of the men, undaunted by the demise of Alan and Jim, had begun to get into formation in the lights of the cars. They formed a semi-circle, facing out at the other parked cars, all of them staring defiantly at the unnatural, advancing death.

Hundreds of glowing purple lights advanced slowly upon them, accompanied by growling and snapping jaws.

Dave thought he could smell the sea.

It reminded him of happy vacations from his youth. Hunting out the women, wooing them, then leaving them for another one the next night. *Great days!*

Only this wasn't really anything like that.

He had just watched his ex-boss, his good friend, eat one of their deputies, a stand-up guy, Alan Borrowdale. Dave had gone to school with Alan's mother. He had also gone behind the cafeteria with the same woman on several occasions. She was always more than accommodating.

He'd just watched helplessly as the young man shot and killed one of his son's best friends.

They were now reduced in numbers, soaking wet in the incessant rain, and surrounded by hungry ghouls, intent on eating them alive. This was no vacation in the Gulf of Mexico.

'Fire at will. Take these fuckers down now,' he shouted as he picked himself up from the wet floor.

The noise of gunfire was deafening. But the sight of the monstrous beasts surrounding them being cut into minced meat, their rotting flesh splattering everywhere, was satisfying.

The only thing not satisfying was the stink. The stench of putrefied flesh rose in the air, enveloping the smell of the gunfire. It ruined the moment for 'Big' Dave, who, even though he was soaking wet and petrified, was rather enjoying the power he had at his command.

'Keep firing,' he shouted over the roar of gunfire. He grimaced when he heard the empty click of his gun as his magazine ran out. He fished about in his trousers for a second one. As he did, he heard several of the other guns fall silent too. This didn't worry him too much as the ground before them was already littered with a large steaks of shredded freak.

He heard the others discarding their magazines and grinned at the satisfying clicks of new ones being engaged.

Even though his ears were still ringing from the sound of the combined gunfire, another noise caught his attention. It was the same noise that the things had been making before they'd been mowed down by the Uzis. Dave thought it must have been far away, other *things* attracted by the noise and coming in to see what all the fuss was about.

He welcomed them. *Come and get some, you bastards.*

Unfortunately, this wasn't the case.

As he looked about, scanning for more *things* to shoot at, he noticed that the enemy was a lot closer than he'd originally thought.

They were almost right on top of them, or more appropriately, directly below them.

The open jaw of one of the monsters wrapped around his ankle. He hadn't even noticed it was there until now. Its bullet ravaged torso was still functioning, even though, by every law of nature, it shouldn't have been. He watched with confused eyes as a hand that, by everything that was holy and sacred in life, shouldn't be there, grabbed his lower thigh. He screamed as teeth tore through the wet fabric of his trousers, sinking into his flesh, all the way to the bone.

As the thing bit him for a second time, his knees buckled. There was nothing he could do to stop himself from falling into the puddles of the parking lot for a second time. Agony coursed through his body as the wet, bloody gravel came up to meet him.

This agony wasn't in his leg, it was coming from the rest of his body. From everywhere.

The monsters, or the remnants of them, were crawling all over him.

He could feel their strong talons tearing into him, their strong jaws snapping at him, the feel of their dirty teeth, ripping, tearing and...

What?

What the Hell are they doing? he asked himself between screams and garbled shouts.

He knew what they were doing. Deep down, he knew he was being eaten alive by Hellish ghouls, but he also knew his men should be stopping them right about... now!

But they weren't.

Why are there no more gunshots? he asked himself.

Even though he didn't want to admit it, he knew the answer.

All of his men, he thought of them as *his* now, were in the process of being overrun, and eaten, by what looked like the reanimated corpses of the dead.

'Big' Dave Coleman was reminded of an old painting he had seen as a child. It had scared him deeply then, and now, in the midst of being eaten alive by freaks, it terrified him once again.

The painting was 'The Triumph of the Dead' by an artist called Peter Brueghel the Elder. Why that information should pop into his head right now, at the worst moment of his entire life, possibly the last moment of his life, he didn't know.

A shiver ran through him as one of the things bit into his head.

'BRRRRRAAAAAAIIINNNNNNSSSSSS!' was the very last word he ever heard.

31.

THE GUNFIRE DIDN'T just attract more of the shuffling monsters to what was happening in the car park. It also attracted the attention of the students who were inside the barn. There was a rush towards the windows as everyone scrambled to see what was going down.

A cheer erupted as they watched the police form a circle and pump the *things* surrounding them full of flying lead from their submachine guns.

'WE'RE SAVED!' someone shouted, and another cheer erupted.

Jason, however, wasn't celebrating, not yet.

The noises he'd heard in the changing room at the back of the stage, and what had happened to the sheriff and the deputy, had dampened his excitement. He'd seen how easily that rescue had fallen apart, so based on that, he was going to reserve his jubilation, *just for now,* he thought.

Within moments of the celebration, the mood changed. It turned sombre, then downright quiet. One of the deputies stopped firing and shouted something to the others as he began to search his trousers, obviously looking for a new magazine.

A few of the others followed his lead.

What the deputies outside couldn't see, but what the kids in the barn could, was that the monsters, the ones who had been cut down by the gun fire, were not dead.

Not in the truer sense of the word.

'Look out,' Jason shouted as he banged on the windows, hoping to catch the attention of the deputies outside, any of them. He could see what was about to happen, and he needed them to be able to see it too.

As the smoke from the gunfire cleared, it revealed piles of organic debris in its wake. It looked like the back room of a butchers, minced meat with arms and legs still attached, and in more than a few cases, heads too. Unbelievably, to him, and to everyone else watching the events, the piles of debris were still… he didn't know if the word *'alive'* was the right one to use, but it was the only one that his numbed brain could conceive at such short notice.

The bodies were pulling themselves along the puddled, gravelled floor, towards the policemen, who were all loading new magazines into their weapons. Piles of raw, bloody, humanoid hamburger dragged themselves towards their assailants. Some were nothing more than heads with hole riddled torsos, but each and every one of them had snapping mouths and glowing purple eyes.

'Get away. Run. RUN!' Jason shouted. As he did, everyone in the barn turned to look at him. Mercifully, this made them miss the unholy devastation that was about to occur.

The creeping things snuck up on the unsuspecting deputies and swarmed them, snapping, gnashing, biting at everything in their way.

The cops had absolutely no chance.

Before any of them realised what was happening, all sixteen men, from the Sheriff's deputies to the volunteer firemen, had been overpowered, and devoured. Jason and some of the others watched, wide-eyed and helpless, from inside.

He turned away from the massacre and rubbed his eyes.

A complete silence descended over the room, broken only by small, pathetic whimpers and sniffles.

He couldn't believe what he had just witnessed. He looked over at Kevin and Hank, who were flanking him; their faces were empty, devoid of emotion, drained of colour. Their eyes were the eyes of people who had seen too much; they were the eyes of the dead, or at least the dead inside.

'I think we're on our own again,' he whispered. 'We need to get out of here, and we need to do it now while the things out there are distracted.'

Hank looked at him. Jason was buoyed a little by the small spark of light in his eyes. 'Yeah, let's do it. I mean, what the fuck else can go wrong tonight?'

~~~~

The door to the changing room rattled and banged in its frame. The handle shook as something from the other side of the door gripped it, trying to get out.

Suddenly, it stopped.

Everything was silent for just a moment.

Then, the silence was broken by a small *click*.

It was only a quiet sound, one that would have been lost in the general hubbub of the everyday goings on of a high school disco. It was overlooked now too, but it shouldn't have been.

It *was* a significant noise.

It was the sound of the lock, unlocking, from the inside.

32.

THE FEEDING FRENZY abated.

The deputies were dead, eaten. The Uzis they had all been so proud of lay scattered on the floor, useless against the hellish aggressors who were hellbent on eating brains. Some of the *things* had been stopped by the assault when a stray bullet had been lucky enough to pass through their skulls. But, as the deputies—who had loaded up and come to fight an enemy they didn't know—hadn't been told to aim for the heads, they had mostly opted for the easier body shots.

Most of the bullets had passed harmlessly through the army of the dead. Some had been cut in half or had limbs torn away, but this had proven only to be a mild annoyance to the single-minded monsters. All it had done was stop them from getting to their meals that little bit quicker.

These monsters however were nothing, if not resilient, and were determined to get to their meals. Each thing feasted on the brains of the humans as the alien parasites, that were now controlling their bodies, instructed them to do. In the process, they spread their parasite into the new hosts, and therefore expanding their army.

If they were going to conquer this world, then they had to defeat the pathetic species that inhabited it.

They would take Earth, one brain at time!

~~~~

On the outskirts of the parking lot, six figures lurked within the trees. To a casual observer, of which there were none (or none that were still human anyway), these six figures might have looked normal. To another casual observer, they might have looked like the other mutant scavengers that were milling around in the parking lot.

But both casual observers would have been wrong, and both would have been in serious trouble.

The six figures had *once* been human, but they were far from that now. Each had mutated into something else; something *more* than they had once been.

They were no longer the Lion's High School Cheerleader Squad.

They were now Mutant Superhero Zombie Killing Disco Cheerleaders!

33.

WITH THEIR VISION piqued for night-time, due mostly to the second pairs of eyes that had formed beneath their original ones, they peered through the bushes towards their prey. They had been given a mission, a higher purpose, and failure was not an option.

They were tasked with saving humanity, and this planet, from the parasites that were infesting the good people of Kearney. Today it was a small town in Arkansas, tomorrow it was America, after that, the rest of the world.

That was their assignment, and they *would* complete it.

While they had been submerged in the strange mud, the lightning bolt that hit them had not been random. It had contained information, biological information. This information had merged with, and then transformed, the cheerleader's DNA on a molecular level. It had mutated them from mere attractive, athletic cheerleaders, into superheroes. Each had been bestowed a unique talent, one that would aid them in their battle against the extra-terrestrial parasites.

It was now time for these Mutant Superhero Zombie Killing Disco Cheerleaders from Outer Space to put their talents to work.

All six ex-cheerleaders halted their march towards the barn at the same time. The leader, with the extraordinarily large afro hairdo, raised her hand into the air, and the clicking, and the walking, stopped. She pointed towards the parking lot, towards the circle of deputies who were currently shooting at the things they were here to defeat.

When the shooting ceased and the smoke from the guns cleared, they watched the oncoming massacre. Not a single drop of emotion passed on any of their strange faces. Their four, dark-silvery eyes witnessed, in great detail, the horror as it unfolded before them. They knew there was nothing they could do to help the humans with the guns, they were already dead, collateral damage. It was the rest of the town, the state, the country... the world, they had to protect from this deadly threat.

When the attack was over and the deputies were defeated, the girls knew that most, if not all, would reanimate and join the search for fresh brains. It was time for them to step into the fray and halt this infection from spreading, once and for all.

Their mission had begun.

As one, all six girls stepped out of the bushes and into the flooded parking lot. The leader put her fingers into her mouth and whistled. It got the attention she needed. All the ex-humans that had been happily chowing down on the deputies, and all the others still shuffling around the parking lot looking for, and moaning about brains, stopped.

What was left of the music promoter was there, as were the remains of Oldman and Oldgirl. Rob was there too, although he was only recognisable by his clothes, as his face had been mostly eaten away. Razor was there, as were Mr Turnbull and Ms Wellborn, also the thing that had Ms Wellborn's pink panties around its head. The girl from the van, the one who's name no one could remember, was there too. The police force was well represented by Sheriff Hanley and Deputy Pulis. There were well over a hundred others. Good, decent, ex-Kearney residents, all of them in various states of decay. The two things uniting them were their glowing, purple eyes and their insatiable appetites for brains.

None of the monsters attacked the six cheerleaders. It was as if some small, still-functioning part of their brains, knew who, or what, these newcomers were.

A mutual respect passed between the two groups.

But it didn't last long.

The leader looked around the parking lot at the half-eaten bodies of the deputies. She knew there was nothing to be done for these poor souls, they were not what she needed to focus on.

She had no use for dead, nearly dead, or un-dead humans.

Her huge afro hairdo began to swell, becoming even bigger than it had been. She raised her hand in the air, and the five ex-cheerleaders behind her stood ready.

On the same signal, the beasts in the parking lot and the ones in the surrounding bushes all stood ready too.

The fight was on!

34.

Birdie McSwann

BIRDIE COULD ALWAYS be found at the top of the cheerleading pyramid. She was among the smallest girls in the school, but also one of the feistiest. Because she was slight, she was a natural athlete and gymnast. True to her name, at the end of the cheer, she was the one thrown into the air to soar, usually holding the Kearney Lions banner high for all to see, and cheer.

The superhero powers that had been invested onto her were apt to her name. When she climbed out of the charged, purple mud, she had been sporting a very impressive wingspan, and the ability to fly. The large, angel-like wings stretched out a full four feet. The feathers adorning her wings were complete with razor-sharp edges and lethal points.

When Suzi Afro gave her the signal, Birdie McSwann stretched her wings. She lowered her head and rushed straight into the first wave of ghoulish onlookers. She took them by surprise, and the sharp ridges of her wings hit six of them, slicing their heads from their bodies, effortlessly. As the severed heads rolled through the puddles, and the bodies dropped to the floor, another group of ghouls turned to face their attacker.

Birdie saw them coming and stopped. With a primal yell, or a cheerleader chant, there was no longer any difference, she brought her wings back into her body, then thrust them out again.

Hundreds of lethal, dart like, feathers fired from them, shooting out in all directions. The aim of the darts was true, and each hit a target, embedding into the heads of the monsters, changing them into something resembling undead porcupines. Each *thing* stopped advancing and fell, their bodies splashing dead in the mud as they did.

She stretched her wings again and swung herself around. Another four of the beasts dropped as the ridges diced them into thin sliced, undead, cold cuts. She was grabbed from below by a group of undead who had been the victims of the fight with the police. None of them had legs, and they had dragged themselves along by their hands, to get their chomping jaws around the new addition to the buffet. The weight of their grasping hands began to drag her down, and for a moment or two, it looked like she might be losing the battle to stay upright.

She closed her eyes and retracted her wings. She crouched down on her heels, closer to the snapping jaws. As she bent low, the monsters pawed at her, trying to get at the meal that had just opened itself up to them. More upright monsters joined in the melee, all of them vying for a portion of the brains that were on offer.

A muffled scream came pierced the night.

It sounded distant, far away, but getting closer; louder. Suddenly, the scream lost its muffle, and became sharp, ear-piercing. Something erupted from the pile of undead scrabbling over the fallen cheerleader.

It was Birdie.

She sprung into the air, taking the group of attackers with her, some with legs, some without. Undeterred by their sudden height and velocity, they continued to claw and snap at her. With a spectacularly

169

athletic swoop, she soared high, up to a grand height, where she hovered for a moment before reversing her position and swooping back down to earth at break-neck speed.

As she hurtled towards the ground, she dropped her burden of monsters, crashing them to the ground headfirst, killing them, instantly.

With her wings spread wide, she swooped majestically along the carpark, the lethal ridges of her battle-wings claiming many an undead trophy in their wake. Her once pristine white feathers were now dripping with the purple gore of her victims.

Gracefully, she shifted direction and swooped back into the dark, cloudy sky. Once again, she hovered for a moment, allowing everyone on the ground to marvel at her impressive wingspan, before diving back down to earth, landing effortlessly back into formation.

35.

Wendy Whips

DUE TO HER flexibility and light bodyweight, Wendy was a staple of the second level of the cheerleader pyramid. Her thick, dark hair was usually tied in braids and put up into a tight bun. Since their *accident*, however, the bun had fallen. Her long hair now hung down her back like two thick, gorgeous, dangerous ropes. At the end of each rope was what looked like small silver skulls.

As she stood, awaiting instruction, she gyrated her neck, spinning her weapons like a wet towel in a boy's locker-room.

When Birdie swooped back down from on high, Suzi Afro raised her hand, giving Wendy the signal she'd been waiting for, to let loose her wrath on the unholy demons marauding around the parking lot.

Without a second thought, she sprang into action.

Two angry, hungry-looking monsters instantly accosted her, snapping and hissing for brains as they shuffled forwards. With one swift shift of her neck, there was an almighty CRACK, and her two weapons spun forth. In the wink of an eye, severed heads were splashing into the water-logged parking lot, and decaying bodies were crumpling to the floor.

Undaunted by their colleagues' demise, another group of *things* turned their attention to the newcomer. This group included the unholy atrocity with the pink panties wrapped around its head. There were four of them in this advance, and Wendy took them all in her stride, standing before them, inviting them forward.

One by one they came, arms reaching, fingers grasping, desperate to get at the delicious meat and brains on offer from this girl. She cranked her neck, unleashing her lethal hair-whip at each advance. More heads flew through the air, each leaving a purple trail of blood, and pink panties, in its wake.

Four motionless, headless bodies lay in a heap, their heads nowhere to be seen. Wendy was standing in the centre, her hands on her hips, purple gore dripping from her hanging braids. She breathed three long breaths, visible only from the small spray of blood coming from her mouth. As if this was a signal to the monsters, another attack approached.

This time there were more of them.

Almost twenty of the gnashing, rotting, stinking ex-humans headed her way. They came from every direction, surrounding her, hell bent on murder, and eating.

Undaunted, Wendy kept her stance, inviting them forth.

As they got closer, their goal in sight, she began to swivel her head. It was only small circles at first, causing her hair to spin. The closer the ghoulish *things* got, the faster her head moved, and the wider the circles became. Around and around and around her head gyrated, creating a vortex from the two skulls at the bottom of the braids. The skulls began to rise, and her hair became a deadly sawblade.

The capacity of the beasts to think beyond brains was extremely limited, proven by the fact that they all continued to advance, regardless of the deadly perimeter of spinning hair. As they got closer, Wendy hunkered down on her heels, waiting for the things to get close. Seconds before the first one entered the deadly zone; she began to rise.

The rapidly spinning skulls at the tips cut through the monster's feet, then their shins, then their thighs. As she rose, the sawblade cut through their midriffs, chests, and finally, their heads. Most of the twenty or so monsters that had joined the attack had been reduced to pink, green, grey, and purple sludge as her hair tore through them like they were nothing more than rotting fruit.

She continued to rise, her feet leaving the floor, propelled by the up spin. That was when the blades on the soles of her feet slipped out of the pumps she was wearing. They briefly gleamed in the lights from the barn before she kicked out at the remaining monsters, tearing through their necks with powerful, well aimed thrusts.

Once all the monsters in this attack were fallen, she landed back in her position. She took herself a bow, and slipped easily within the formation of the cheerleaders.

36.

Nicky Nunchucks

NICKY'S NATURAL POSITION within the pyramid was next to Wendy in the second tier. Once again, she was slight of frame but powerful in her abilities.

After she was submerged in the purple mud, Nicky emerged with a pair of horns growing from the top of her head. But they were no normal horns. A thick chain ran between them, with hand grips on either one.

As Wendy landed next to her in the formation, she looked towards Suzi, waiting patiently for her signal to begin her mission. Once it was given, she strolled, confidently forward, towards a group of *things* that had been loitering around the main door of the barn. They had been rattling the doors, trying to get inside, and therefore missed the excitement of what had previously gone down. When they saw her approach, their attentions were switched from the potential meals inside the building to the easier option approaching them.

As one, they turned and began to advance upon her. Shuffling, growling, and groaning; demanding her brains for their delectation.

Nicky was ready.

The drooling monsters edged closer. She stood her ground, waiting for them to come to her. She was ready to make her move. Small, shallow breaths escaped her as she posed a defensive posture in the rain. Slowly, she reached up towards her head, grabbing the antlers growing there. She dislodged them with the ease of someone well practiced in this manoeuvre. She removed them and held them out before her, allowing her enemy to see what she was holding.

They didn't care, or perhaps they couldn't comprehend what they were seeing, either way, they continued to advance.

The horns and chain began to spin. Forwards and backwards they whirled as she swapped them from front to back, from hand to hand, in ultra-quick, ultra-impressive, movements.

Completely unimpressed with her skilful display, the monsters continued hobbling forwards, towards their fortuitous meal.

With a flick of her wrist, a loud crack, followed by an ugly sucking sound, and one of the monsters' heads was ripped from its body. The thing fell abruptly, unnoticed by its colleagues, into the mud, water, and blood that comprised the parking lot.

Nicky stood upright, her nun-chucks held out before her in the same defensive stand, holding one handle while the other was tucked underneath her arm. To the untrained eye, she hadn't moved a muscle.

There was another SWOOSH, and another head, complete with a spray of purple blood, went flying off into the night.

Still, to the naked eye, Nicky hadn't even blinked.

Two more SWOOSHES claimed two more heads, but still the horde of undead advanced upon their intended meal. Nicky, as calm as could be, slotted the strange nun-chuck-horns back into her head and beckoned the advancing menace towards her.

As they drew closer, she flicked her arms, and they became disjointed, expanded, and elongated. The bottom half dropped at the elbow. They very nearly fell onto the waterlogged floor of the parking lot, just stopping short of the muddy, bloody puddles.

The extended arms were held together by what looked like chain.

She began to twist them around and around and around. As her arms spun, so did her body. Like a spinning top, she swirled forwards, into the advancing monsters, ripping arms, legs, and heads from decrepit bodies in her wake. Blood and gore flew in every direction as she mowed the rotting, but dangerous, beasts down one by one. Thick chunks of zombie littered the parking lot while bloody splatter covered the windows and doors of the barn.

Once she was finished on her mission, Nicky's arms returned to their normal length, and covered in a thick sheen of purple gore, she calmly slotted back into her position alongside the other girls.

37.

Pamela Pummels

PAMELA HAD ALWAYS been a big girl, bigger than most of the boys on her block when she was growing up. She was never teased about this however, for two reasons. The first being the obvious. Even the bigger boys on her block feared her, she could fight like the best of them. Some of the older boys had found themselves in sticky situations where they had come off second best to a girl in the park. This was not good for their reputation on the block. The second reason was because she was gorgeous! She found from an early age that hardly anyone wanted to fight, or tease, beautiful girls.

She was the strongest member of the cheerleading squad and therefore spent most of her time holding up the other members in the pyramid, or she would be the one to throw the lighter, more agile girls in the air.

Since coming out of the mud, Pamela had grown. Her already muscular frame became even more so, and her strength was accelerated, ten-fold.

On the signal from Suzi, it was her turn to get in on the zombie killing action.

She noted that the deputies and firemen, the ones who had arrived late to the party and had not wanted to hang around, were all now getting up again, reanimated as half eaten, hungry monsters. Pamela saw it as her duty to rid the world of these particular parasites.

As quickly as the putrid men stood up, she knocked them down, wading into them with her ham fists.

There was no holding her back.

As former Deputy 'Big Dave' Coleman lunged himself at her, his jaw snapping at her neck and head, she clenched one massive fist. The punch came from somewhere close to the floor and gained close to supersonic speed as it swung upwards, towards his head. The *clonking* noise as her fist connected with his chin was comical, the destructive force behind it was not. She simply knocked the big ex-deputy's head clean off.

She looked the blood that was dripping from her fist, threw her head back and laughed, hard.

Another ex-deputy became reanimated. He got up from the floor, and after a quick sniff of the air, began to shuffle towards her. One punch from the ground, once again catching it directly underneath the chin, and another body, sans-head, was sent flying. This body flew a fair distance before gravity took its hold and it began to fall. The head, however, continued to rise, leaving a purple, bloody trail behind it like a grisly comet, or the world's worst firework.

Pamela kept on going, punching, hitting, and kicking absolutely everything in her path. If they were undead, then they were in big trouble. It wasn't long before the whole group of former deputies had been beaten into the pink and purple pulp they were made of. She made one-hundred percent sure none of them would ever rise, looking for brains, again.

When they were all gone, nothing but undead juice smoothie, she made her way into the trees surrounding the parking lot. She had noticed, peeping through the branches, were more of the purple eyed monsters.

The other cheerleaders witnessed her progress into the wilderness, watching, emotionless, as bodies—some in greater states of decay than others, some clothed, some naked, but all of them headless—were tossed from the bushes into heaps between the cars on the parking lot.

A single whistle from Suzi was all it took for Pamela to stop her pummelling, and emerge, bloody but smiling, from the trees to make her way back into the formation.

38.

Betty Bootie

ALL THE BOYS called her Betty Bootie. It was widely understood that her booty was the best booty in the whole town, maybe even the whole Tri-State area. When she tried out for the cheerleading squad, it was the most attended trials the small high school had ever seen.

Not only did she have a fantastic booty, but her athletic prowess was second to none. She could flip, toss, somersault better than anyone in the cheerleading squad, the school, maybe even the state. Her prowess had been noted by talent scouts for team USA. Olympic gold medals might have been in her future if not for the inconvenience of the accident and, of course, the subsequent mutation.

Her upper body strength was second only to her lower body strength. So, when the strange purple lightning went looking for assets to enhance, it found them easily.

When Suzi signalled for her to step up, she did with much aplomb. She flipped out of formation, sailing high over the heads of the other girls.

A group of the purpled eyed beasts had amassed by the trees on the opposite side of the parking lot from where Pamela had caused so much carnage. Betty landed on the wet ground with such grace she hardly even caused a splash. She crouched straight into another spring, jumping high into the air, spinning to gain more momentum. She landed with her muscular, and tanned legs wrapped around one of the unsuspecting *thing's* neck. With a wink and a short, sharp twist of her hips, her legs tightened, and the monster's head came off in her grip.

As the decapitated monster crumbled brusquely to the floor, she landed with finesse. Without even a pause to catch a breath, she sprung forwards, pushing from the floor in a flip. Propelled by her strong forearms, she launched herself at another of the bewildered beasts. Her both feet planted firmly in its face, knocking it to the floor. As it fell, she went with it, landing with her feet still in its face, resulting in a sickening, wet crack. The grotesque abomination instantly stopped moaning and complaining.

Within a moment, she found herself mobbed by several of the creatures, all of them reaching, scratching at her, trying to grasp their pound of flesh and brains.

As she was besieged, she fell backwards and was instantly beset upon by several *monsters*. They scrambled on top of her, trying their very best to get some purchase on her, whipping themselves into a frenzy of excitement at the potential serving of fresh brain.

The other cheerleaders watched as she succumbed to the overwhelming number of attackers. They flinched, ready in an instant to help their fallen comrade. Suzi raised one of her hands, telling the other girls to hold tight. They looked at her, but the confidence in her face infected them, and they all relaxed.

For a few nervous moments, they watched as the melee of *things* mewled around, groping, and fumbling for a slice of the grounded superhero.

None of the other girls breathed.

Then, from the middle of the pile, something shot into the air, It left a crimson trail behind it.

It was a head.

It was an ex-human head.

The purple glow in its eyes was flickering, faulting. Its mouth was snapping, but the thing was more than obviously dead; really dead.

The head was soon followed by another.

The sight of the second calmed the squad of cheerleaders. They knew Betty had the situation under her control.

With an ear-piercing scream, the other *monsters* that were scrambling around in the pile fell backwards. Something large, something that wasn't just a head, shot out from the centre of the ruckus.

It was Betty, and she was holding several objects in her grip.

They were heads.

She soared high through the air, holding the crania by their hair, leaving a crimson trail in her wake. It was a beautiful sight, but on closer inspection, it was comprised of blood and decaying flesh.

As she reached her zenith, she threw the heads down, towards the pile of fallen monsters in the parking lot, cracking more than a few skulls in the process.

She landed in the centre of the writhing bodies and continued to flip, spin, and pirouette. With careful and considered movement, she took more of the monsters out, knocking them to the floor and quickly, and acrobatically, decapitating them with her arms and legs.

Once she was finished, she looked back towards her squad of superhero cheerleaders, wiping a thick swatch of gristle from her face, revealing her grin.

Suzi signalled her to come home.

Betty Booty did as she was beckoned.

39.

Suzi Afro

SUZI WAS THE BADDEST cheerleader in the squad. She had all the moves. She was strong, graceful, athletic, and a natural born leader. All complimented by her having easily the best hair in the whole of the county.

Fact!

It was one big-assed curly afro.

She was also a beauty, rocking the Cleopatra look that all the boys craved, with her mocha skin and big dark eyes; it made her the envy of all the other girls. Now mutated into a superhero disco cheerleader, her four dark eyes saw everything. She could see every move the monsters made, and she could relay those moves back to her squad.

But her superhero power didn't just extend to foresight. She had another skill under her belt.

Or above it, as the case may be.

As Betty made her way back into the formation, Suzi was surveying the situation. Her girls had done a fantastic job of cleaning up shop, but she knew it wasn't over. There were still others out there, lurking in the trees and hiding in the bushes. Her job was to lure the last of them out.

She strode out into the middle of the corpse strewn parking lot and held her hands in the air. 'Come at me, you muthas,' she shouted, turning a full three hundred and sixty degrees. She beckoned the rest of the monsters, taunting them to come at her, daring them even. 'I've got the brains you're looking for, bitches,' she continued.

The rest of the girls watched in fascination as hundreds of bright purple dots appeared within the trees. The growling and the shuffling became louder as they drew into the clearing of the parking lot.

'BRRRRRAAAAAAIIINNNNNNSSSSSS!' they hissed, purple eyes blazing as they spied their next victim.

Suzi stood her ground, her arms still raised as her hands summoned the cannibalistic brutes to join her. Her large afro was pulsing like there was something alive within the confines of the beautiful mass. Something that was itching to get out. The rest of the girls saw it, and each of them smiled as instructions from their leader entered their heads.

From the trees the things came. There were increasingly more of them, hundreds, probably more.

Despite their kill rate, the girls were still heavily outnumbered.

None of this seemed to bother Suzi. She had the scenario figured out in her head.

Literally.

As the murderous monsters advanced, she knelt into the puddle infested parking lot and signalled her girls. The call was telepathic, silent. No-one else heard it except for her squad, and as she knew they would, they all responded, immediately.

As one, the girls rushed towards their leader and lined up behind her. Suzi closed her eyes, and once again, her hair danced as if there was something alive inside it, trying its best to get out.

The huge, pulsating hairdo parted.

Inside the dark rack was a gun.

It was an Uzi.

It was one of the Uzis the deputies had dropped after they'd been attacked. Birdie McSwann was the first to reach into the hairdo and retrieve one. Expertly, she checked the magazine and chambered a round before stepping to one side.

Wendy Whipps stepped up next and retrieved another submachine gun from within the magical hairdo. Then Nicky Nunchucks, Pamela Pummels, and Bettie Bootie all took their weapons.

The Mutant Superhero Zombie Killing Disco Cheerleaders from Outer Space with Uzis were ready and primed for action.

'OK, girls,' Suzi said, standing up and holding her own gun. 'Fire at will.'

All six girls fired into the bushes, the trees, the cars; anywhere they could see the glowing purple eyes of the monsters. They were knowledgeable about these beasts and knew to go for the headshots. The noise of the gunfire was deafening, but consistent. Only when the last of the monsters fell from of the bushes, onto the parking lot, minus their head, did they stop.

The smoke from the hot guns clouded the lot, and for a moment, the girls kept their poise, silhouetted in the gunfire haze, ready for more glowing purple eyes to come forth from the foggy, wet night.

None came!

They'd done it.

They'd saved humanity from the invasion of the purple brain eaters.

40.

AS THE SMOKE cleared, the parking lot was littered with decapitated bodies, bloody puddles, and mounds of pulp. The undead were once more *just* the dead. The immediate area resembled a battlefield from a post-apocalyptic war film.

The rain had stopped, and a cold wind was blowing across the field of death. The only movement was a stray pair of bright pink women's panties, caught in the wind, pulling cartwheels over the strewn cadavers.

Suzi surveyed the scene, making sure nothing had survived.

Nothing had.

She then diverted her attention to the barn.

Girls, the barn, she broadcasted telepathically. As one, the girls turned their attention towards the large building. *This was the Purple Brain Eaters' destination, there must be humans inside. They'll need our help.*

The girls regarded the structure as if it was something they should know. Maybe it was somewhere they had been before, in their past lives, before their superhero mutations had taken hold. Suzi knew there were people inside, she thought it might be someone she knew, or had known… or was supposed to know. Maybe it was someone she had once cared for! As quickly as it appeared, the thought passed, and all that remained was an overwhelming urge to help.

Birdie, Wendy, open the doors and free the humans trapped inside.

Without question, the two mutated cheerleaders made their way towards the huge barn doors. The rest of them stood, awaiting orders.

The doors were locked. Birdie attempted to open them, first with her hands, then with her wings, both to no avail. Next up, Wendy gave it a go, whipping her dangerous thick hair against the wood, to see if there was any give. There was none.

Locked, from the inside, Suzi transmitted. *Pamela, get that door open. The humans inside will be terrified of what has happened out here tonight.*

I'm on it, the big girl replied through her own thoughts.

As she stepped up to the porch, she tested the doors, finding them indeed locked from the inside. She looked over at Suzi with a question on her face and in her mind. *What do I do now?* she asked.

Suzi just nodded.

Pamela received the instruction she wanted with a return nod before turning her attentions back to the doors. She clenched her fists and lowered her left shoulder. The wrecking ball that was her hand dropped almost to the floor. With an almighty roar, she swung as hard as she could. As the ham-fist struck the wood, there was an explosion accompanied by an ear-splitting crack. Thick splinters of wooden panels tore through the air, towards the girls who were watching.

Suzi's hair stretched out into a net and caught the hazardous splinters before they could do any damage to her girls.

Pamela stepped away from the gaping door and looked back towards the squad. As one, clicking their fingers in their formation, they followed Suzi up the steps and onto the porch. There, they stopped, and Pamela fell back into position.

Without hesitation, Suzi leaned into the gaping hole that used to be a door.

The lights were on, but there was no sign of anyone in the foyer. 'Humans,' she shouted, her voice sounding like the amalgamation of hundreds of different voices, all saying the same thing, at the same time. 'You are safe from the purple brain eaters.' She stepped away from the door, expecting an onrush of scared teenagers to blast past her at any moment.

It never happened.

They must be in the back, scared out of their human minds, she sent to the girls. 'Humans, we are here to help,' she shouted again.

Once more, there was no reply. She shrugged towards her squad and closed her eyes to use her gift of third sight. Nothing was coming through.

She gave her girls the signal to follow her.

As they stepped through the splintered door, the interior of the barn was silent. Not a sound was to be heard except for the striding of their own feet in the debris of the wood. The second door, the one that led into the main hall, was also closed. Suzi reached out and gripped the handle. She gave it a twist, but there was no give in it. She closed both sets of eyes and contemplated the door. Once again, she could read nothing that was behind it. *Lead paint,* she thought to herself. *Stopping me from sensing what's inside.*

She had no idea if this was true, but for some reason it sounded plausible to her, and she accepted it.

She moved backwards and motioned for Pamela to step up and do her thing. The big girl gratefully accepted.

As she clenched her fist, ready to pummel it against the door, a small clicking noise caught her attention. She looked down in time to see the door open, just a tiny crack. She stepped away from the door and looked to Suzi. She too was looking at the door as it opened, just a fraction, with a squeak.

Pamela backed away.

The door fell open again, just a little bit more this time.

As Pamela slotted back into position, Suzi reached out and touched the handle. The metal was cold, but as she was now a mutated superhero, temperature meant nothing to her. She pushed it open, just enough for her to see into the hall.

In the centre of the room, in between the tables and chairs that had been pushed to barricade the windows and the doors, stood a boy. His skin was much the same colour as her own, and he looked to be about the same age. He was dressed in a dirty white suit with a dirty white waistcoat and a black shirt underneath.

Jason?

The word, or question, flashed through her head for only a brief moment before it was gone, and the boy was a stranger again.

He turned as the door opened, and Suzi saw his eyes were blazing a brilliant bright purple.

For a moment the flicker of recognition was mutual.

Then the boy screamed. It was a loud, unholy, piercing shriek, and all the windows in the barn smashed as one. The six superhero cheerleaders covered their ears and crouched to protect themselves from the incoming shards of sharp, broken glass.

A thunder of footsteps overtook the scream as the dominant noise, as from behind the stage came the shuffling of at least a hundred pair of feet.

~~~~

Suzi had been knocked backwards from the impact of the scream. She looked up from her prone position, oblivious to the slices and cuts that the shattering glass had caused her skin. She would have deployed her hair to protect her girls, and herself, from the glass but seeing this boy had knocked her senses awry. Her squad was behind her in much the same state as she was. Cuts and slices, but nothing permanent, nothing life threatening.

The biggest threat they faced, right now, was the one-hundred or so purple brain eaters shuffling towards them, leering at them, hissing, moaning, grasping. The glow from their purple eyes cast eerie kaleidoscope shadows on the floor as they advanced, reflecting from the shards of broken glass that were strewn everywhere.

A strong arm slammed into her shoulder, and she felt it grasp her, pulling her up from the floor. She turned, ready to fight whatever it was, whoever it was, but to her relief, Pamela was smiling down at her. She nodded, and all her girls behind her nodded back.

Then they turned towards the horde.

The monsters faced the girls, and the girls faced the monsters.

Once again, small flickers of recognition passed between them. Birdie recognised what was left of Brad in the crowd. As he looked at her, for a split second, the purple light in his eyes dimmed, and what was left of his brow ruffled. The same thing happened between Hank and Betty and Nicky and Kevin. Wendy and Pam looked around the room, but there was no sign of either of the boys they should have recognised.

Suzi stepped forward, towards the leader of this group. His face twitched and sneered. His mouth snarled at the hand that rose to gently touch his face. His facial tics stopped as her hand caressed his pale skin. Her fingertips lightly traced his jawline. The purple light in his eyes, that was blazing only moments ago, flickered, and something like a smile spread across his bluish lips.

~~~~

The boy raised his own hand towards the girl's face. His smile completed as he touched her skin. There was a memory, it was something deep within him. He knew who this girl was. She wasn't just a brain for him to consume, she wasn't just meat, or even a mutated freak with big hair and four eyes, who had been changed with the sole purpose to kill his kind.

To him, she was something more. She was someone...

A noise from behind her killed the moment.

One of the girls had spread her wings. The feathers on the wicked ridge of them were sharp as daggers.

At that moment, everything changed.

The dimming light in his eyes began to blaze once more, and the vicious tics of his face, the snapping of his jaws and the twitch of his lip, returned with aplomb. Without any further warning, he snapped at the hand that was caressing him.

~~~~

Suzi recoiled, just in time. She saw Birdie stretch her wings in her peripheral vision, and she also saw the purple light flash back into the boy's eyes. Whatever had passed between them was gone. The boy changed from something resembling a human, into a thing with an insatiable appetite for brains in the blink of one of her of her eyes. She stepped back, out of his reach. As she did, he raised his head and screamed.

'BRRRRRAAAAAAIIINNNNNNSSSSSSS!'

The other monsters, standing, twitching behind him, as if waiting for instruction, took this as a command and began to advance.

The six girls took their defensive positions, flexing muscles, spinning hair, twirling arms, and ruffling feathers, as the encroaching undead surrounded them.

The stench of rotten meat and curdled milk was almost overpowering. It was invading the girls' personal space as the ugly, hungry mouths snapped, and the dangerous taloned hands scratched at them.

There are too many of them. Suzi pushed her thought out to the others. *We need to fall back. We can't win this fight in here.*

The girls looked at each other, not believing what their leader was telling them to do.

'But...' Nicky replied. That was all she could bring herself to say.

I said fall back, that's an order!

As Suzi backed away from the horde of purple brain eaters, she clicked her fingers. The other girls, each shaking their heads, obeyed her instruction.

In formation, the six Mutant Superhero Zombie Killing Disco Cheerleaders from Outer Space (with Uzis), backed out of the hall, making their way into the rain-soaked parking lot.

The monsters, sensing victory in their battle with the superheroes, followed them.

When they arrived in the parking lot, they stopped and turned towards the ghouls, who were literally falling over themselves to get out of the barn. There, they stood their ground, and watched as wave after wave of monsters burst out of the broken double doors. The gnashing and the gnarling were deafening as the hungry beasts rushed—or rushed as much as mindless, undead freaks could—towards them.

The girls took up their defensive positions once again. Each willing to give their very lives in pursuit of this victory and the successful conclusion of their mission.

A moment passed between them. It was a sweet moment where they all remembered what it had been like before the mutations had taken hold. Back to the innocent time, less than a few hours ago, before the dead had arisen, when all they had to worry about was if they chipped their fingernail polish while performing their cheerleader routines.

A single thought flashed through each of their heads. It was a thought that sounded both ludicrous, and genius, at the same time.

The thought was... *PYRAMID!*

Without over-thinking it, Suzi, Pamela, and Betty dropped to the floor. Nicky and Wendy climbed onto their shoulders. Without further invitation, Birdie McSwann climbed up, via Pamela and Wendy, and perched on the shoulders of Wendy and Bettie. When they were all in position, they stood up.

The brain eaters stopped their advance and looked towards the odd formation before them. If it was possible, they looked more confused than normally. Seeing this erection appear before them was not something their limited brain capacity was ready for; it was most unexpected.

'LI-ONS... HEAR US ROAR,' Suzi began to chant.

'LI-ONS... HEAR US ROAR,' Pamela and Wendy joined in.

'LI-ONS... HEAR US ROAR,' Nicky, Bettie, and Birdie continued...

'LI-ONS... HEAR US ROAR, LI-ONS... HEAR US ROAR, LI-ONS... HEAR US ROAR...' they chanted in unison.

Another thought flashed through their heads.

If looks could kill, girls. Remember your killer smiles, Suzi shouted, telepathically. *Killer smiles!*

They all knew what they had to do. They had done it before. In fact, they had been famous for it as high school cheerleaders, back when they were human, before they'd changed.

It began with Suzi.

She smiled.

That was all it took.

It was a broad, wide, perfect smile that displayed both rows of gleaming white teeth. The teeth were in perfect contrast to the filthy, green, crooked teeth of the monsters they were facing. A flash issued from her mouth. It was dazzling, far brighter than any moonbeam, maybe even brighter than the sun itself. It stunned the beasts before it, and the advanced guard raised their rotting arms to shade their burning purple eyes from its brilliance.

The glow didn't stop there. It spread along the bottom row of the pyramid. It passed from Suzi, through to Pamela in the centre, and then to Bettie at the other end. It then spread upwards. First Nicky smiled, and Wendy followed suit. Finally, when Birdie joined in, it was as if a circuit had been fully connected.

The brilliant light shone brighter from Birdie's mouth before passing back down through the other girls, one by one, before returning to Suzi. The pyramid pulsed a perfect white. It lit the sky, it illuminated the parking lot, it cut a swathe through the thick, rolling purple clouds. The stars were visible for the first time that night. The sick purple glowing from the brain eaters' eyes dulled in comparison with the pulsating pyramid.

Six beams stemmed from the structure, one from each cheerleader. The beams joined in the centre, forming a single point. Then, with an almost biblical wind, the light zapped through the heads of every single brain eater in the parking lot. Killing them instantly.

They dropped as one. Jason, Brad, Bruce, Mr Smart, all of them. The purple lights in their eyes dimmed before flickering out, as if they had never been there in the first place. Each monster crumpled to the floor, unmoving, dead, but for good this time.

Only when the last of them had fallen did the brilliant light from the pyramid flicker out.

Each girl, each Mutant Superhero Zombie Killing Disco Cheerleader, dismounted the pyramid. They looked to Suzi before slipping back into their triangular formation.

There, they stood, surveying the rain soaked parking lot, basking in the glory of the slain bodies of every single dead looking fuck.

41.

THE NIGHT WAS dark, and the sky was moody. The clouds rumbled and rolled over each other, darks crashing into the lights like a mighty deity was attempting to mix oil and water together… and failing miserably.

Six, strange young women stood, covered in blood, in a corpse strewn parking lot. Each of them was staring into the sky. The leader of the squad, a mocha skinned girl with an unusually large afro, and two sets of glowing eyes, looked around her. The guns, the Uzis that had been discarded by the girls after they had massacred the undead, began to disappear as her hair began to pulse and grow. *We'll need them later,* she thought to the others.

They all agreed.

Suddenly a break in the clouds allowed a shaft of burgeoning morning light to filter through the miserable morning scene. It was glorious in the dying light of the horrible night. However, it didn't last very long as something dark, much darker than the night the girls had just witnessed, loomed in the shadows behind the clouds. It was big, and it was not of this world. Maybe it was not even of this universe. A single gleam of sunlight broke through the clouds, reflecting off the metallic hull of the strange vessel.

The girls knew what it was. The spirit that had entered within each of them, the one that caused their mutations, given them the superhero powers, the ones they needed to save humanity from the purple-brain-eater infestation, knew what it was.

It was the enemy.

An enemy that needed to be defeated.

They knew the invaders would not rest until the planet had succumbed to their power, until every human had been enslaved, and all the riches and resources harvested for their own greed. They would send more dumb slaves to ensure humanity was beaten. When the last human was a shuffling, undead moron, the invaders would slip in, strip the planet, and move on, leaving an empty husk in their wake.

The extra-terrestrial essence within the girls had seen it before.

Not this time, Suzi vowed looking at her girls. *This time, they will not win.* 'Ladies,' she said in her commanding voice. 'Shall we?'

They all smiled before climbing back into their pyramid.

Birdie gave a yell and gripped the two girls beneath her, who in turn gripped the three girls beneath them. As she flexed her wings, the pyramid rose from the ground. Birdie flapped and rose higher and higher from the wet, bloody scene below.

She had her orders, as did the others.

They all knew their destination.

The fight had moved onto the spaceship above!

D E McCluskey

42.

AS THE PYRAMID of Mutant Superhero Zombie Killing Disco Cheerleaders from Outer Space (with Uzis) ascended towards the Heavens, they had only two things on their minds. The first was to battle, and destroy, their enemy... and the second was to look damned good doing it.

Epilogue

AS THE NATIONAL Guard, the fire department, and the ambulances that had been ordered on behalf of the, now defunct, County Sheriff's office arrived on the scene, none of them could believe what they were witnessing.

It was carnage, complete and utter devastation.

There were hundreds, maybe thousands, of decapitated bodies, arms, legs, heads, guts, intestines, some other stuff that no one could identify, scattered everywhere, all over the parking lot. The barn where the Lions were having their District Championship dance was deserted, the smashed doors swinging in the wind.

Each man and woman who disembarked from their vehicles gazed upon the scene with a sickened awe. No-one, not even the few servicemen, and women, in their ranks who had seen active service in various locations over the years, had ever seen anything like this.

The stench was terrific, and more than a few of the younger, less experienced service staff added to it by vomiting up the contents of their stomachs.

'Jesus Christ, that must have been some party,' was all that was said, muttered by a young ambulance driver as he shook his head. There was not even a trace of humour in his expression.

A large man wearing the uniform of a firefighter saw something that caught his eye. He bent over and picked it up. As he held the item in his hands, he recognised it. It was something he had seen before, plenty of times. He looked out towards the trees beyond the parking lot, searching for something, anything that would give a clue of what had happened in Oldman's barn.

With a sigh, he dropped the pink panties back into the puddle he found them in. He shook his head and started the long, arduous job of attempting to identify the many bodies strewn around the parking lot.

D E McCluskey

To my knowledge, the small town of Kearney, Arkansas doesn't exist, and if it does, this is purely a coincidence. I just wanted to get that out there.

So…

Let's rewind a few years. Let's go back ten years, no… make that twenty. No? OK then, shall we say thirty-eight?

I'm ten years of age! I'm scared of my own shadow. I'm still having problems coming to terms with the *glow in the dark* Muppet stickers on my wardrobe door. My sisters have messed with my head for years, whispering through the wall to me as I lay, scared stiff, in my single bed, pretending they were Tinkerbell, telling me they've been watching me for Father Christmas, making sure that I've been behaving myself. Add to that all the Irish Catholic guilt that had been heaped upon me from a young age, and you have an idea of the formative years of D E McCluskey.

No wonder my brain has turned into the twisted quagmire it now is, dreaming up tales of people addicted to running over other people's heads, falling in love in a zombie apocalypse, heavenly serial killers, and ghosts that want to disembowel their victims.

So, there it is, laid bare, for the whole world to see.

It was about this time that my cousin, up there in bonnie Scotland, introduced me to a new world. A world that changed me for a while, up until I started to notice girls and learned about heavy metal music. He introduced me to the world of comics.

Men bitten by radioactive spiders; billionaire vigilantes dressed like bats to intimidate the bad guys. Men and women with fantastic abilities teaming up for the greater good.

My own golden age of comics…

These days, it's all about the films and TV series; half of the kids don't even know that it all started on paper that would rub off onto your fingers and make them black, or red, or blue. My big question was, if the guy who got bitten by a spider could get the properties of the spider, then could the kid who got the ink rubbed into his skin develop the properties of the book?

I guess it did.

Thanks, John, I don't think I would have taken this route if you hadn't let me sit and read those comics for hours on end, all those years ago in the Braise…

So, a little about this book!

Firstly, I want you (the reader) to not see this as a book at all. I want you to see it more as a bit of fun. I want you to indulge me and read it as if you were thirteen years of age, watching your first cheesy horror film, one that had been made in the 1970s or 80s. I want you to think of special effects made before the dawn of CGI and the awful (but awesome) acting where the girl screams with her hands over her mouth while looking at the camera as the zombie, who is obviously just a man with eggboxes glued to his face and covered in tomato ketchup, shuffles after her, shouting (all together now):

'BRRRRRAAAAAAIIINNNNNNSSSSSS!'

I met Stephen Harper a few years ago; he is a top bloke with a shit load of talent running through his heavily tattooed being. His artwork is phenomenal, as I hope you have appreciated in the superb cover for this book. Another thing about him is his knowledge and enthusiasm for anything horror, grindhouse, sci-fi, exploitation—I could go on—is second to none!

I got working with him and a company called Slumberjack Entertainment (Peter McKernon and Rod Hay) on a film anthology called *The Micro Killers*, (I wrote one of the segments called "The Comedian"), and I gave credence to the idea of writing this book as a screenplay and

203

getting a small budget together and making it into the B movie that I so want it to be. Stephen, Peter, and Rod read the poem (as it was originally), loved it, and as I write this, we are still considering it!

I had written it initially (once again) as a poem that I was hoping would make it into one of my Interesting Tymes comics. But I deemed the content a little too 'adult', as that series is meant for children. So, I expanded the story into how I would want to see it on the small screen, filmed on VHS. It became the novel you have (hopefully) just read.

Mutant Superhero Zombie Killing Disco Cheerleaders from Outer Space (with Uzis).

It is what it is…

A bit of fun!

~~~~~

So, this is the bit where I say my thanks to all the people who helped, and had a hand in, dragging this book from a crazy, stupid idea into a crazy, stupid novel.

First off, as always, I need to thank Tony Higginson. A long-term collaborator, whose advice I see as GOLD.

Forsaken Folklore (Ste Harper) is an artist who resides in Liverpool UK. Known for his unusual, imaginative illustrated - portraiture, he has contributed works to numerous book and comic covers. Film posters, conventions, festivals, exhibitions, magazines, to name but a few.

For all enquiries please contact:

forsakenfolklore@gmail.com

https://linktr.ee/Forsakenfolklore

Proof-readers for this nonsense include... Christina Eleanor, Tara Lane, Charlie Moor, Hayley Louise Dougan, and one of the long-termers, Natalie Webb (she was hanging on for TimeRipper).

The last, but certainly not least, proof-reader is Lauren Davies. Not only does she do the very final read through, but she has to put up with me and my varied mood swings too... If only writing was easy, eh?

Lisa Lee Tone edited this madness into something coherent and readable. All the Americanisms used in the book, and all the cultural references, she helped me with. It's not until you try to write something based in Smalltown, USA that you realise the absolute gulf between our two nations, not only in language, but in the way the language is used... Anyhow, she fixed it all up for me, and I'm eternally grateful.

Big thanks go out to Ann McCluskey, Grace McCluskey, Lauren Davies, Sian Davies, and rest of my fantastic and loving family! (Everyone in Secret Santa is getting a signed copy of this book this year.)

But mostly, and as always, to you, the readers. I always say this, and it sounds as cheesy as the dialogue in this story, but it's true. Without you good people reading, there would be no point in me writing, and if I didn't write, I wouldn't like to think about what I'd get up to!

Thank you all, and I mean it, from the bottom of my dark heart.

Be good to each other, please leave a review of this book, and save the bees!

Dave McCluskey
Liverpool
August 2019

Printed in Great Britain
by Amazon